DRIVE

OR BE DRIVEN

Polestars

DRIVE

OR BE DRIVEN

Stories of Travel

POLESTARS 6

Aliya Whiteley

NewCon Press
England

First edition, published in the UK April 2024
by NewCon Press
41 Wheatsheaf Road, Alconbury Weston, Cambs, PE28 4LF, UK

NCP320 (hardback)
NCP321 (softback)

10 9 8 7 6 5 4 3 2 1

ISBN: 978-1-914953-69-9 (hardback)
978-1-914953-70-5 (softback)

Cover Art by Enrique Meseguer; cover design by Ian Whates
Editing by Ian Whates and Donna Scott
Typesetting by Ian Whates

Contents

Early Bird

Get in the car.

Start the engine. Back out of the drive. Leave the house behind.

The road is alight in the dawn, a scarlet blare of a morning. Flip down the visor, squint so you can just about see. There is a deep pothole, you know it well, with a square sprayed around it in white paint: a warning, a promise. Avoid it. Start off in silence, aware of the sanctity of the early hour. Everyone else is still in bed. You picture them lying splayed, duvets pushed back in the heat, woken by your engine, waiting for you to go by so they can turn over, return to sleep.

Take the back road, looking forward to the empty straight of the motorway. You pride yourself on your early starts, and of the peace that greets you as you travel to the city. But this morning you reach the slip road and find it full, and the three lanes beyond it, too, all full, cars inching forwards, almost at a standstill. There must have been a crash. Or perhaps there's an event in the city, there's nothing on the sat nav, maybe take a different – no, it's too late, you're on the slip road now, crawling into a space between bumpers, and it takes time to even reach the main carriageway. A car in the middle lane pauses to let you in, and you work your way to the outside lane.

This is going to be a long day.

Turn on the radio.

Someone is speaking. Telling a story. One ends. The voice says **The End**, then another starts. It's short. It feels incomplete. Another story. One after the other. Characters come and go, arrive, leave, having feelings, saying words. The events of each story feel pointed. Arrowed at you. You are involved. Your ears are necessary. These characters are nothing without you. You give yourself to it.

You would love to arrive, reach the city. Have a coffee. Find your desk. The sun is no longer low and red in the sky. Flip up the visor. The voice goes on speaking. It travels from past to future, occasionally brushes over the here and now with a light touch. The cars in front of you edge forward, and the ones behind you move closer. You try to keep in the flow, moving in time. You look around, idly, at the central reservation and see tall weeds there. It occurs to you that nobody is travelling in the other direction. Those three lanes are clear. Silent.

The cars in front of you all contain one person, a driver, and you look at the backs of their heads, the sides of their faces. They are intent. You think they're listening to the radio. To the stories. You're all hearing the same stories. Where are you going? The voice on the radio tells its stories, and you're in the flow of traffic, it's dangerous, the days get so hot, the road is so fast even when we all can't move, so stay in the car, okay? Just stay in the car.

Drive or Be Driven

She met Ioan at an icebreaker for their hall of residence. He invited her back to his room, along with the other students on their floor. They squeezed into the space and drank vodka from paper cups. He had a partner already – a presence captured only in a silver photo frame on his desk. It was a glamour shot, posed, in black and white. The face did not seem, to Margaretta, to be attached to a body.

Everything in Ioan's room, three doors down the corridor from her own, looked as if it had always been there: the photo frame, the laptop, the posters. He even had a car, with an allocated parking place opposite his window. The things he possessed were marked, known.

Margaretta engineered her time to leave the hall of residence whenever he did, and he noticed it, and offered her a ride up the hill, to campus. During that first short journey she watched his hands on the wheel of the Citroen, not hearing anything he said. He parked up, and she climbed from the passenger seat and staggered away feeling battered, confused. She realised later she had not said goodbye, so she knocked on his door, late that night, to thank him and to apologise.

'I was a bit worried,' he said, leaning in the doorway. 'I wondered if you weren't feeling well.'

'I'm good,' she said. 'I'm just rude.'

'Well, any time you need a lift…'

'How about every day?'

He took in a breath, his head tilted back a little. His hand was on the doorframe.

'I'll pay for half the petrol,' she said, then, 'I told you I was rude.'

He laughed. She wanted him to know her, mark her.

The latest tipping point was announced to have passed at the beginning of November. They were in his car. The news came over the radio, on the hour, as he was manoeuvring into a space on the back street behind the science building. There was always a slot available for him.

Margaretta was not in the least surprised. She had watched her parents lose their farm piece by piece to dust storms, droughts, and heat events throughout her childhood on the continent; this affirmation that time had run out to solve the problem only made sense to her. But Ioan turned up the volume and listened to the clip of the UN speech about timelines and oceanic extinctions with the expression of a boy concentrating in class, preparing to take a test later. She felt something different for him then, in his apparent innocence, and wondered how he could have kept it intact for so long. It was this country, on the west of the island, so wet, raised from the sea and still dense with green life. The roads were at the beginning of disrepair, lumpy and broken in some places. All was verdant, forcing up through concrete cracks, but not enough to change the way he drove, not yet.

'That can't be it,' said Ioan. 'They'll come up with something.'

'I don't have a lecture until ten,' she said. So they sat, side by side, while he went through all the stages of grief at once. He made a joke about it, months later. February, maybe. *Anger, bargaining, denial: I did the works,* he said, and laughed. Distance makes even the worst things lose their power to wound. The country, like Ioan, carried on. The horizon was not yet visible.

By March, the second term, they were good friends, best friends.

He told her his car was a DS3. It had 88,000 miles on the clock but when Ioan had bought it (from a dealer his father knew) it had been an old lady's car, barely used. *One careful owner.* The car hadn't let him down yet, and he repaid its loyalty with his care. He didn't ignore his responsibilities: oil changes, tyre pressures, warning lights. He had a name for the car. It was called Wellington.

They'd fallen into the habit of driving at night with the windows down, out of town to where the streetlights stopped and the plant life began. Margaretta found it joyous to be cold in the night breeze, deafened by the clash of the engine with the wind. April moved into May and the heat mounted. Ioan would drive fast, and they rarely saw other cars on the back lanes he favoured. If someone was coming the other way, it was nothing more than a blinding moment – then he would slow down and dip the headlights. The change in the glow made the land look condensed, syrupy. They would squeeze past and he would build speed again. They did not turn on the radio or listen to music. There was only the rhythm of the engine, and the tangle of her hair in her mouth, a little open, open to the world.

One night, in May, he parked in a layby in the middle of nowhere, next to a farmer's gate with a dirt track woven into the land beyond.

'I've ended it,' he said, as soon as he'd turned off the engine, his hand still on the key. He left the sidelights of the car on, and the field beyond looked like a film set, an unreality into which an event might spring. 'It wasn't working. She's so far away, I haven't seen her in months. And she says she's not coming home for the summer. I haven't even really thought about her, though. That's the thing. When she said she'd made it through to the last round on the Safe Havens project, I didn't feel anything. They're taking her. She found out today. And she said we could – we could get married and I would get accompaniment rights. That's so old fashioned, I can't believe they still offer it, but they do. I checked online.'

'You don't want that?' Margaretta said, to the windscreen, to the view of the gate, as if there was an audience beyond. If she could have been accepted to the Safe Havens, she would have gone without a backwards glance. High ground, protected ground, up in the Arctic circle. She hadn't made the first cut.

'It was the way she said it. Like it was a duty. To… protect.'

'You?'

'Not me.' He sat in silent thought, then said, 'The emotion. To protect her idea of love. But we haven't been in love for months. Not since…'

Since what?

She wondered how he could be so certain to speak for someone else's idea of love. She knew she'd given herself the reputation of being rude. Did she dare to ask him? It was agonising, to not speak, to not ask. Her desire to know how he defined such things was painful.

He surprised her, deep in her indecision, by lifting his hand from the gearstick to touch the central vent of the dashboard, his palm to the plastic slats. He always wore a ring on his little finger of that hand. It was a thick band of silver that sat only just below the knuckle, and she said, 'Where did you get that?'

He moved his hand back and pulled at his finger until the ring came off, with difficulty. For a moment Margaretta thought he was going to offer it to her. Instead he flicked it, with precision, out of the window. 'Gone,' he said. When he unclipped his seat belt and reached for her, she was ready, her hand quick to her own belt release, prepared to meet him halfway.

*

The picture frame was missing.

Maybe it was in one of his drawers, Margaretta thought. For him to take out and look at when the urge arose.

Study continued as usual. They were both busy with exam preparation throughout June. The end of their first academic year was approaching. Her lectures were sweaty and long. She took to arriving early to try to get a good spot under the air conditioning in the library. She told him about it, but he never joined her there. Their places together consisted of his room, his car.

Ioan began to collect old scientific journals from fifteen or twenty years ago. He ordered them online and they arrived, via courier, in big piles that he organised chronologically and kept under his bed.

'Isn't all the science out of date?' Margaretta asked.

'I want to see how it's changing,' he said. 'The science. Our understanding of it.'

He took to bringing a few magazines along on their drives, and he would read articles out loud about the climate fight. It was magical to her: his voice, his effort to encompass, understand. Through him, she could almost believe in finding solutions. Then he stopped getting the magazines delivered, and when she looked, they were gone from under his bed.

Maybe he had thrown out the picture frame after all.

Or there hadn't been a girlfriend.

It could have been a picture from a magazine, long discarded, snipped out and placed on his desk. It had never looked real. But why pretend such a thing?

Once the thought came to her, she could not get rid of it.

In July, the few weeks left before term ended, the heat was intense in the day and did not drop much at night.

She got into bed with him every night, after their drive, but woke at three a.m. as if an alarm had been set. Time: gone. She lay there, watchful, feeling the heat of his body pressed up against hers in the single bed. Sometimes it became a bright fire that she couldn't bear. She took to getting in and padding down the corridor to her own room to take deep breaths in her own darkness.

The end of the academic year was upon them. He would return to his parents' house until September. It was close, only an hour away. She would stay at the university. She had decided not to risk the trip home. Flights had become sporadic, often cancelled, or interrupted by protestors. She would have had to get three separate boosters for the variants, and upon return there would be checking and rechecking of that paperwork. Questions, delays, queues. All of it felt deliberate, to stem the rising tide of humanity.

At least the exams had all been taken and passed well, and the promise of another funded year of study was secure. It had been earned; it could not be taken away. She held on to that thought, the solidity of it.

On their last night together, he drove them out of town and took a left turn, not a right. There was no gradual change to the rural. The roads widened, and they joined a stream of other vehicles in which his Citroen was unremarkable. It slotted well into the flow of traffic, and she felt as if it was taking them towards something rather than moving away from it.

'Where are we going?' she said. She realised she had never asked him that question before.

He switched on the indicator, the slow tick from the dashboard familiar to her, and pulled into a slip road that led to an industrial estate. A board had been set up at the entrance, showing a map of black and white spaces.

'We're here,' he said.

Traffic lights dictated their pace: wait, go, wait, go. Further in among the featureless buildings, the closed business fronts and the shuttered warehouses, there were no people, no other cars. They were alone, in a secret place. It was not so different from the turning by the farmer's gate. The car contained them, held them, was impregnable.

At a speed barely above walking pace they took a turn, passed through an alley, and an empty area opened before them: a vast car park with white lines fading, asphalt cracked. Beyond it lay the hulk of an abandoned factory, maybe. Some sort of industrial building that had housed many at work, in the grip of fervent production. The windows were smashed, all of them. Graffiti, careless tags in blue and black, marked the walls.

'Plastics plant,' said Ioan. He parked up between two just-visible lines, facing the factory, then switched off the engine, leaving the headlights on. She felt as if the whole building might move, shift its weight, groan, and start to sink. The ground could have swallowed it and she would not have been surprised.

'Are you my girlfriend?' he asked her. 'I want to get home and say to my parents – she's my girlfriend. Tell them about you.'

'What would you tell them? That I'm a rude foreigner who makes you spend too much money on petrol?'

'Yeah, I'd probably lead with that,' he said. He put a hand on the dashboard vent, just like before, and she put her own hand on top, and said, 'You want to give it a name?'

'Why not? Girlfriend and boyfriend. Like back at school. Holding hands in the playground. Did the kids in your school used to do that?'

'Is it that kind of world any more?'

'It could be.'

'We're together.' She didn't know why she was resisting. She took her hand away, and he let his drop.

'It's so hot,' Ioan said. 'All the time. You must have grown up in it. The heat.'

'It was different. A different kind of heat. I can't explain it.'

'Wetter? Drier?'

Margaretta told him a story, instead, about the time her parents' farm had been invaded by stink bugs, brought in their thousands on a southern wind, blown over the house, the crops, the animals. The air was black with them at first. Then they settled and began to eat, and mate, and everywhere bore their smell. The sound of them, crunching under her feet: she would always remember it. It wasn't possible to move without killing them en masse, making her a murderer.

'What happened?'

'We hired an industrial vacuum and sucked them up,' she said. 'At least, the ones in the house.'

'Do you miss it? The farm? Your home?'

'No.'

'How come?'

'It's not there now.' Aware that sounded melodramatic, she added, 'Really. The farm is not there. That land, those crops. My parents moved into the city when the insects and the droughts got too much.' It was not exactly true; the buildings were still there, she supposed. They hadn't managed to sell the farm, had ended up abandoning it, so it was only a home for the beetles, the weeds, the ones who came after, uncontested now, better suited to this new world. Margaretta pictured the tractor, locked in the largest barn, a padlock and chain on the slatted wooden doors. When she was very young she had found a gap in the slats at the back, pushed her way through and climbed up on one huge wheel, struggling to reach the cabin, managing to swing back the door. The interior had possessed a warm, comforting smell of work, of her family's sweat. If she travelled back to that barn, made that hole large enough to admit her, and climbed up into that tractor seat once more, it would no longer comfort her. No, what she said was true, after all: the farm on which she grew up was not there any more.

'What will you do? At your parents' house?' she asked Ioan.

He stuck out his chin, his gaze fixed on the rear-view mirror. 'Work a few shifts at the service station, make some money, see my old mates. Miss you.'

She smiled. It was still half a joke. She pictured her face in the picture frame, propped up by his bed. A black and white version of her, caught in a pose. A head without a body. She could become part of that old bedroom, forever reserved for him, no matter when he chose to come and go.

'I might sell the car,' he said. He patted the steering wheel.

'Really?'

'My dad says his friend has got a Sapling in. Electric. A bargain. It'll save me a fortune in petrol. Better for the planet.'

'That makes sense,' she said. 'How long have you had this one?'

'A few years?'

'Aren't you... attached to it?' Was that a ridiculous question? It felt stupid, but it was pertinent, it meant something.

'It's just a car.'

'Not to me!' she said. She couldn't believe she'd said it out loud. She was so good at not giving anything away.

'So you only like me for the car?' The joking tone continued, and she was grateful to him for it. It made everything easier. She realised gratitude was her overwhelming emotion. 'You did warn me you were rude.'

'Yes,' she agreed. 'I did tell you that.'

'I'll show you a picture.' Ioan took out his phone, tapped away. The image on the screen was of a grey car, only a shade darker, perhaps. It was compact, pert. She couldn't see much of a difference. If this was the future, it looked exactly like the past.

'It's cool,' she said, aware she was using the wrong word, but not certain what the right word was. She hated it when her grasp of English deserted her. All around the world, people were losing things. It was a fever that was spreading. The study grant and the passed exams bought her two more years, at least. Then there were schemes – not the Safe Havens. But other opportunities. And Ioan would not let her go.

'Could you love someone who drove a Sapling?' he asked her.

'I think maybe I could.'

Margaretta touched his arm. He was solid, the muscle strong and smooth. She would give him a photograph of her, to put in his frame. He would return in a few months, and things would go on, the same. No matter the make of car, she could be driven.

Luisa Opines

He first came when my aunt was not at home.

I opened the door to his knock. He had a smile prepared; it was a good one, with teeth. 'I'm asking questions,' he said, and pointed to a badge he wore. It was purple, with white writing on it, and next to that was a picture of him. 'It's for a survey.'

'My aunt will be back later,' I said, 'I can tell her you called round.'

'Actually,' he said, 'I can ask you. If that's okay?' And I was flattered, in the way that only the young can be when given sudden attention by a stranger.

I did not invite him in. I was not that stupid. But it turns out a lot can be said on a doorstep.

He produced a small rectangular device from a black case. The flat surface glowed. 'My tablet,' he said. 'It's all technology nowadays.'

'What does it do?'

'Haven't you seen one before?' He seemed surprised, but held the tablet out so I could see it clearly. 'I can record your answers by touching the screen. See?' He began to touch the screen, his fingers fast and agile, his long nails tapping on the glass. 'Right. Here goes. What do you think the crime rate is in your neighbourhood?'

'I don't think there is any crime around here, is there?' I said. We lived in the deep dark wood, my aunt and I, with nobody nearby for miles and miles. I'd never felt unsafe, even for a moment. Boredom was my usual emotion.

'Nothing at all?' He frowned, and tapped the screen.

'Unless you count the animals,' I joked. 'They're up to all sorts, I bet.'

He laughed. 'Of course,' he said. 'Plenty of murder and mayhem there. Right. Can I ask you – if the crime level went up, would you think about relocating to a different neighbourhood?'

I pretended that the house and the decisions belonged to me. It came quite easily to me; I was at that age. 'Yes, I think I would.'

He nodded. 'Wise,' he said. 'And what if the crime level dropped? Would you feel safer then?'

'Well, it can't drop. I'm perfectly safe.'

'Yes,' he said. 'Sorry. Stupid question.' He swiped the screen, and smiled again. 'Right, that's it. Thank you for your time.'

'You're welcome.' I couldn't see that I'd been any help to him, and that bothered me. I wanted to produce the kind of answers that filled pages and pages of surveys, but I didn't know anything and hadn't been anywhere. All I knew was the cottage. I wasn't even allowed to go out gathering berries and mushrooms with my aunt. And now the most exciting thing that had ever happened to me was about to end.

'One last thing,' he said.

'Yes?' Oh, I was so eager. My heart breaks for the girl I was.

'Can I come back next week with a few more questions? There are new surveys popping up all the time, you see. '

'You must be busy.'

'It's a living,' he said. 'Is that okay?'

'Yes, that's fine, although I don't know much about anything, I'm afraid.'

'Oh, you'll be perfect. You were a big help today. Can I take your name for the records?'

'Luisa,' I said. 'Can I ask *you* a question?'

'Hah! You're getting in the swing of this. Yes, of course. Ask away.'

'What's your name?'

'It's Peel.' He pointed to his badge again, and stepped a little closer so I could read it.

FOREST INFORMATICA – it said, in bold letters, and underneath that, next to a picture of him, his name: PEEL.

'See?' he said, and I did. I saw his picture and his face, and the smile on both, and I liked it.

He asked me so many questions over the months that followed, always arriving a few minutes after the departure of my aunt. She would put on her cloak and head out into the forest, and I would wait in a state of high excitement for the knock at the door which would always follow. He had immaculate timing.

'You're in a good mood,' my aunt would often say, when she returned home to find me humming as I washed the floor, or did one of the many tasks she concocted to fill my days.

'I am,' I always agreed. 'I really am.'

She was happier too, I think, because I'd stopped asking her so many questions of my own, such as where my parents were and whether I could go with her when she left. I had a fresh purpose. Peel.

'On a scale of one to five, how do you feel about holidaying in hot countries?'

I really wasn't a fan of them, even though I'd never been anywhere, so that turned out to be a one.

'If you were to open a savings account, what rate of interest would you be looking for?'

Once he'd explained the concept of a savings account to me I opted for at least one point five per cent.

'Indicating your choice on the screen, what shade of green do you find most attractive in a frozen pea?'

I particularly liked the questions for which he held out the tablet towards me. I touched the screen, with authority, no matter what I knew or didn't know. The nonsensical nature of the things he asked me were no barrier to my belief that I had become important. I imagined he belonged to a place where all of these questions were relevant, and I came to feel that if I gave enough answers that pleased him, he'd ask me to go back there with him.

'What qualities do you look for in a soft drink? Touch all the words that apply.'

I opted for tasty, refreshing, sparkling, and non-fattening.

His shoes were always grey suede, and he wore trousers and a shirt that were as black as his swept-back hair. He was both young and old. I felt he understood me as an equal, but he could have commanded me and I would have obeyed. I wanted to impress him with my answers, but how could I do that when nothing had happened to me? I wished for an event to come along and make me more interesting.

And then an event happened.

My aunt did not come home.

I sat at the table and picked at my fingernails until the sun had set. Then I opened the door and stared out at the night. The dark trees seemed closer, thicker. Their leaves hissed in the wind with ominous intent.

I had no idea what to do.

The first question Peel had ever asked me came into my mind, along with my blithe reply. There is no crime, I had told him. Was that true? What did I know about it? Just because fear and pain had not burst through my door, it did not mean that it was not waiting for me to come to it.

Something huffed, in the night. Something took a breath.

I slammed the door and ran to my bed. I pulled the covers over my head. I would not sleep, it was an impossibility; I would never sleep again, I could never sleep ag-

Knock knock.

My eyes opened to the bright light of late morning, filling my bedroom. For a moment I was peaceful, wondering why my aunt had not woken me to start my many duties, then my heart crashed, and I sprang up to run to the door, thinking she must be home, she had lost her key, she had been hurt but was now back, and I threw open the door to find Peel standing there, holding his tablet out with the screen facing me. Upon it were written two words, in thick black letters:

DEEPEST
SYMPATHIES
'We're so sorry,' he said.
'What?'
'Your aunt. We're so sorry she's missing.'
'But I –'
'Word travels fast in the forest. We're all thinking of you.' I'd never seen him without a smile before. Instead he wore an expression of intense sympathy, giving him wrinkles around his forehead and mouth, and between his eyes. It made his skin look loose, pouchy.

'Can you help me find her?' I said.

'Of course. I'll put out the word right now.' He turned around the tablet and began to tap on it.

'I meant – can you come with me, if I go and look for her? Please?'

'Trust me,' he said. 'This will help.'

I watched him at work, his fingers fast, his expression so serious. All I wanted was for him to take over, to say – *quick, pack some food and water, grab supplies, lock up the cottage, I know a place where she might be, this way, follow me* – but he didn't.

'I should go,' I told him, told myself.

You're in a good mood, she had said to me, many times, and I had agreed. She had felt happy because I was happy.

'Really?' said Peel.

'I have to try to find her. I owe it to her.'

'Wait,' he said. 'Before you set off, can I ask you a quick question? It's for the latest survey.'

'I'm not really –'

He turned the tablet back to face me once more. 'Could you indicate on the screen what expression best represents your current emotional state?'

Four little cartoon faces: Happy face, sad face, surprised face, angry face. I reached out and touched the sad face. It was blue, with two tears rolling from the downturned eyes.

'Thanks,' he said. 'Right. Well. I'll leave you to it in this difficult time. Thoughts and prayers.'

'I'll find her, though,' I said, but all I could think of was how useless I was, and how little I knew of that great big forest out there: the one that Peel moved through.

'Well, good luck,' he said.

He really wasn't going to offer to come with me.

I closed the door, and tried to decide what I should pack.

Where to go when there are no trails, no clues?

I now know the answer to that question. I did not move in any direction that could be found on a compass, so much as move towards hope. I could not say if it took me in a straight line or round in circles. The path outside the door soon petered away to nothing so I abandoned the pretence of following it. The cottage was swallowed up by the trees behind me, and the dim rays of light that managed to break through the thick leaves gave me no indication of where the sun sat in the sky. There were only the dense greens and browns of plants and earth. I saw no animals at all, and for that I was grateful. But I imagined their eyes upon me.

I forced myself to call out as I walked, and the forest swallowed the sound.

'Aunt? Auntie?'

Eventually my throat grew sore, and then it began to close over. I stopped calling out, and searched her out only with my eyes.

Nothing.

I stumbled down a grassy hillock and found older, thicker trees with wet ferns clustered around their trunks, and thick patches of mushrooms growing in abundance between them. Could this be the very place my aunt visited every week to collect our supplies?

'Aunt!' I croaked.

It was no good. Not a trace of a footprint, not one broken frond to show she might have passed this way. I collected some mushrooms and put them in the basket I carried. It was getting dark quickly; the day was coming to an end. *Be brave*, I told myself. *I must be brave.*

The biggest tree had split in its middle to create a small hollow, just wide enough to crawl into. It was not much, but it offered more protection than simply lying on the ground. I got down on my hands and knees and crawled through the slimy mushrooms to slip inside, on the damp earth, as the last of the daylight disappeared and a profound blackness settled over the forest. There was only my breathing in the cold air, and the hard ground, and the webs of the spiders and the creaking of the wood. But soon it seemed that the sounds were becoming rhythmic and soothing, and the ground and air were growing warmer, softer, and I realised nothing was my enemy, and then I slept.

'Knock knock.'

I woke. What is it about the illusion of waking peacefully, as if one is still in a warm, safe bed, only to have the real world come crashing down? The soreness of my body was sudden and agonising; I was balled up tight in the tree, covered in slime trails, with a snail on my cheek. I picked it off and struggled out of the hollow.

Peel stood there, amidst the ferns, looking clean and handsome, his white teeth gleaming. 'Hello,' he said. 'How would you feel about answering a question?'

'Not half as good as I'd feel about a hot bath and some breakfast,' I told him. 'How did you find me?'

'No sign of your aunt,' he said. 'That's sad, isn't it? Sad.' He made his sad face, and the skin of his cheeks and forehead sagged. 'Will you be going on, or turning back?'

'I don't think I know which way is back.' I picked some mushrooms, and ate them with some of the bread I'd packed in my basket. It was a chillier morning.

'Onwards it is, then.'

'Was that the question?'

'Ha! Of course not!' He produced his tablet and turned the screen to me. How bright and soothing it was in the dim light of the forest. 'Right. Which of these qualities do you most value in a hand soap? Choose all that apply.'

A floral scent
Antibacterial properties
Creamy lather
Long-lasting bar
Value for money
Natural ingredients
Ethical packaging

'What's ethical packaging?' I asked.

'Can you trust it?' he said, after some consideration.

'Can I trust the bar of soap?' It wasn't a quality I'd thought about in regard to soap, but I selected it, along with the creamy lather and natural ingredients. Three seemed like a good number of things to choose.

'Thank you so much,' Peel said. 'Have a great day!'

'Wait – did you hear anything? About where my aunt could be?'

'I'll check...' he said. He tapped the screen. 'Not yet. But I will. Have a little faith.'

'Fine,' I said.

I picked up my basket and started walking. When I looked back over my shoulder, Peel was nowhere to be seen.

The second day of searching was both worse and better than the first. My illusions were at an end; I would not find her. And wasn't she the woman who had kept me tied to chores, refused to tell me my history, failed to prepare me for the world? Perhaps she had decided to leave, and never return. I would not have put it past her.

I did not really know her at all.

You're in a good mood – she had said. And then she had been in a good mood too. I hung on to that thought above all others.

Onwards, onwards. I came across a dappled clearing with a cheery stream rushing through it, and I washed, and drank my fill of good clean water. The trees shrank back beyond, and I emerged into a field of tall wild flowers of blue; I ran through it with abandon, my basket swinging, to plunge into the darkness once more. Part of me despaired even while I began to see the forest through fresh eyes. It was not a place of fear and cruelty. It had beauty within it.

Then I came across the body.

The blood, smeared over the trunk, had a strong smell to it unlike anything I had come across before. I stopped walking and stared at the mess ahead. It was a body, yes, a body in pieces, ripped apart. An arm, separated from a shoulder, and legs broken and splayed. Panic overtook me. *Auntie*, I thought, and fell to my knees, but then I saw the hooves and the fat under the pink flesh, and I realised it was not human, but pig. A pig had been killed here, dismembered with great force, by something large. Something powerful.

I got to my feet. I took small, slow steps backwards, and retreated until I could not smell the blood any more.

And so onwards in a different direction, until the light began to fade.

It was going to be a much colder night. Already I could feel the icy fingers of the night on my skin. But there, up ahead, like an answer to a prayer, was a rocky outcropping with a gap between two boulders, just wide enough to admit me. I clambered up and lowered myself in to find a small cave with a mossy floor – and even a blanket, waiting for me. How could that be? There was no answer, but I refused to worry myself about the blanket until the morning. I pulled it around myself in the darkness, and slept the sleep of one who has walked too far and seen too much.

'Knock knock.'

I knew who it was before I opened my eyes. When I climbed from the cave, blanket and basket in hand, there he was, looking as handsome as ever.

'Good morning,' he said. 'I have great news! The question of where your aunt might be was raised as a survey yesterday, and eighty-four per cent of people didn't know. Five per cent claimed she was dead, and eleven per cent claimed that her disappearance was a hoax.'

I barely listened. The morning light had revealed the blanket was not a blanket at all. It was my aunt's cloak. I stood there, holding it, half-expecting her to walk up and take it. But there was only Peel, smiling at me.

'What's that?' he said.

'It's hers. Her cloak.'

'No,' he said, 'Really? Hang on, I'll tell everyone.' He took out his tablet and tapped on it.

'She must have slept here,' I said. 'Why would she leave her cloak behind? I don't understand.'

'I'll ask around, see if anyone knows.'

'That's not going to help,' I told him. 'And I should get going. She can't be far away.'

'Before you set off, could you tell me what you think of this statement? *A nearly professional standard of home decorating can be achieved by a DIY approach if the right materials are used.* Strongly agree, agree, neutral, disagree, strongly disagree?'

'No more questions.'

He held the tablet up to my face, 'Easier to answer it than to opt out,' he said. 'It takes an age to opt out. Lots of forms to fill in.'

'I'm not – fine, then.' I touched the screen, randomly, not caring where my finger landed, and he stepped back.

'Thanks,' he said. 'More walking today?'

'Yes,' I said, shortly. I couldn't remember what I had ever liked about him. He looked good, and said the right things, but when it came to action he was useless. I shook out my aunt's cloak and put it on. It was warm, red wool with a silk lining, and I was grateful for it in the cold morning air. But I couldn't help but think of her without it. Freezing. Hungry. Desperate.

Or maybe not. Maybe she was already back home, now, and I was the one who was lost.

'Good luck!' called Peel, as I stomped away.

Where did I come from?

I thought about that question as I forced my sore legs to take me onwards.

In one sense, I had come from a cottage. It was so far behind me, the path to return unclear. I might never return.

In another sense, the place where I had come from was just an invisible to me. I had no idea who my parents were, and if I did not find my aunt, I would never know.

When I find you... I vowed. The words sounded in my mind, in time with my footsteps. *When I find you, I'll make you tell me. I'll make you take me home.*

Wrapped in her cloak, I felt closer to her than ever before. Surely she was close. Surely I would get my answers.

On through the forest, everything familiar and yet strange, no way to tell where I would end up. How big can a forest be? What lies beyond it?

A cottage.

A perfect little cottage, situated in a clearing, stumbled upon as if by accident, as if by design.

It was not my cottage, but it was very like it. It had the same oak door and neat square windows, and the same blue paint on the sills. But it was too clean and new. It looked unlived in. And it was, perhaps, a little too square on the windows, and the paint was just a shade too bright.

I approached the door in silence. I knocked.

'Come in!' called a voice I knew.

I turned the handle and went inside, into a parlour so very like, through a kitchen almost the same, to a room almost identical to my aunt's bedroom.

There she lay, tucked up in bed, smiling.

'It's so lovely to see you, Luisa, dear,' she said. 'I hope you're in a good mood. You know I love it when you're in a good mood.'

'Stop it,' I said.

The smile dropped from her face. The skin around her mouth and eyes was loose, pouchy. 'I don't know what you mean,' she said.

'Come out of there right now.'

'But it's me! Your aunt!'

'Do you think I'm an idiot?' I said. I threw the basket at the thing in the bed, and it put up its hands, and said, 'All right! All right. I'm not your aunt. I admit it.'

'You killed her.'

'I did no such thing! I eat pigs, not humans. Besides, we're friends, aren't we? Friends don't eat each other's relatives.'

'Are we, Peel?' I asked. 'Are we really friends? Come on, get out of that disguise.'

'Fine,' said Peel. He put his hands to my aunt's hair and pulled, and the skin rolled away in one piece. But the handsome young man I was expecting to see was not underneath. Instead I found myself face to face with a great grey wolf, still tucked up in bed: its mouth fixed in a permanent grin, its teeth long and white, and its black eyes filled with sharp intent. 'Well,' it said. 'Now we can see each other properly. Are you scared?'

'No,' I said.

'Honestly, on a scale of one to five, where would you place your fear right now?'

'If you didn't kill my aunt,' I said, 'why do you have her skin?'

'I made it. I created it from the answers to the questions I ask. She loved to answer questions too, you see. She would await my knock at the door, on the moment after you fell asleep, every night. We used to have a fine old time together.' He held up one huge hairy paw. 'And I swear I don't know where she went. She never breathed a word about leaving to me. It doesn't matter, anyway. I have her thoughts and feelings, her likes and dislikes, right here.' He held up the discarded skin: an aunt-shaped costume for a wolf to wear. It rustled, a little, and let out a small whine.

'She really did leave me,' I said. 'I don't understand it. I thought she loved me.'

'Perhaps you never really talked to her,' suggested Peel. 'You never asked her the right questions.' He threw back the bed sheets and stood up. How tall he was; his ears nearly touched the ceiling. He scooped up the skin and crossed the room on his wolf paws; I shrank back as he passed by me to open the wardrobe, revealing a strong white light inside. 'Come on,' he said. 'Come right this way while I hang her up.'

He stepped into the wardrobe and I followed, and we were both in a long corridor, stretching far into the distance, lit very brightly by no light source I could see. Two long silver poles, running horizontally on either side of us, gleamed like the screen of his tablet, and skins, many skins, hung from the poles on hangers. The corridor could not possibly have been inside the cottage; I felt that it wasn't in the forest either, but was part of some other world where everything was sharp and cold and very flat.

We walked, side by side, into that world, until he said, 'Here we are.' He stopped beside an empty hanger, and put my aunt's skin back upon it. Then he took down the one next to it, and I saw it was me. I recognised myself straight away. Peel climbed inside, and in a blur the illusion of my skin became a reality. He was me.

'I'm really not a fan of holidaying in hot countries,' he said. 'And hand soap has to have a creamy lather.'

He was not a murderer, but he was a thief.

'Why?' I whispered. 'Why?'

31

We walked onwards, down the long corridor, until we came to a metal door with no handle. 'In here,' he said.

I've been here ever since. In the other world, the world of wolves in costumes made of questions. They wander around in the brightness, asking each other odd things, telling little jokes, sometimes shouting out strange statements, pretending to be human. Sometimes they band together, all the ones who share a certain opinion about hand soap or foreign holidays, and swagger around arm in arm.

I'm lost amongst them.

Occasionally I see myself in the crowd, and I call out, 'Help!', but my skin turns and plunges back into the crowd. I think maybe Peel doesn't recognise me. Perhaps I don't look like myself any more.

I don't know who I am, just as I didn't know Peel, and I didn't know my aunt. But here, here in the wolf world, everyone is so easy to know. They have their straightforward answers ready to so many questions that don't hurt to think about. It's easier to be certain about things here.

I've been asking myself: on a scale of one to ten, how much would I like to return to the life I had before, in the cottage, trying to work out where I belonged?

I'm not certain. I'll need more time to think about it.

Cold Trade

A planet unnamed. Others have found nothing here to trade with. But we are the crew of the famed Artisan, and we are the best of bringers. We give and take all over this universe. We arrived with intention, took our ship under the ocean, and dived, and dived, and found them. The giants.

But what can we sell to these silent markets of the sea? What can they sell us?

The giants are silent miracles of the water, growing heavy on the nutrient-rich murk. They are four, five times the size of the Artisan. Ovals with fins and a tail and a long mouth. No eyes. No responses, beyond feeding, beyond the endless circles they swim in.

The further up into the shallows we go, towards the light of the three suns, the weaker and smaller the inhabitants become. Above the water: nothing. Not a living thing. Everything taken, nothing to give.

We will find a way to trade with them.

Our ship is equipped for all eventualities. Considerable skills have gone into its upgrades over time, paid for by luxury goods and services from trades numerous. But staying at this kind of depth, under great pressure, is inadvisable. Not for the marvellous ship, which can withstand any environment as long as the safety checks and procedures are performed, but for the stress it places on the crew. For this reason there is a deadline we have set ourselves. Six sleeping cycles, no more.

Tav still feels guilt. She has expressed it often enough. *It was a mistake*, she said, over and over. But what can we say? Zeal and I reassure her. *No blame. Only sadness.* It is something the old bringers say, after a death. I never thought I'd find use for it, but it seems some words only find their meaning through experience.

Do the giants feel sadness? I have looked out at them from the viewing room, the thick transparency distorting their straight mouths into downturned edges, so that it would be easy to think they're in the grip of emotions. Loneliness, too, for they never come together. Each one is separate, travelling its circular route to their own timetable. They avoid all contact – for fear of injuring themselves? Or others? But there must be a time or place when they meet, if only for the continuation of their species. They create curiosity in me – what does the Artisan create in them?

If it could be construed as a peaceful, or blank, existence, then that is not accurate either. A current builds in the depths, a rhythm. It swells to a crescendo and then all turn and face into it, and ride it, angling their fins and tails until it ebbs away. The ship does this automatically too, and in those moments I feel a camaraderie with the giants, and what they live through. This is some sort of battle for survival, perhaps. The desire to keep on living, to turn to the challenge ahead, and meet it. I think I understand.

And from this vantage point inside the Artisan I have seen one perish, and understood that too.

It did not turn to the rhythm, and it began to tumble, over and over, in an exhausting spin. When the swell ended it fell gently, slowly, down to the ocean bed, and did not move again. Then the water lit up, glowed around it, and the skin and flesh of it melted away and was gone. Nothing left. The other giants did not show any interest.

Did I imagine this? It was as if it had never existed. And so it goes, after death. There comes a point where the living have to wonder if they dreamed the way the dead once were.

No blame. Only sadness.

Nothing we offer holds any interest for them. We have sent out samples of food, of entertainment. We have played music and made shows of light in their darkness. On they swim, in their endless pattern.

I have a favourite giant. I have named it Bounce.

If I could establish rules for barter with any of them, I think it would be Bounce, who makes a regular stop at a spongy part of the ocean floor, thick with rough growth, on the lip of a symmetrical hole that seems to be a vent from which the pulsing waves erupt. Bounce lets its long body land on the sponge, and then springs up, its tail upturned as if in joy.

I have programmed the Artisan to arrive at this hole in time to see Bounce, six times a cycle, every cycle. It is utterly regular. *What goes around, comes around:* the old bringers say at the meetups, the ships in their thousands dotting space like stars into the distance. It is to remind us all to trade fairly, but it works here, too, where the giants make their circles, and so do we.

Zeal catches me in the middle of the rotation of these thoughts that will not stop. I'm watching Bounce live up to its name. There it is: the joy. He comes to stand beside me, and we watch Bounce swim away.

'Breakthrough?' he asks me.

Can't he see anything exceptional in Bounce's behaviour? If he won't offer it, I won't take it, so I shrug.

35

'Maybe everyone's right, Filli,' he muses. 'Maybe there's nobody here to trade with.'

'Maybe.'

'We really needed a win.'

I turn to him and hug him, the warmth of our bodies mingling, exchanging. Artisan keeps us at the right temperature but, still, looking out at the water makes one feel chilly. I'm aware we are out of our depth.

When we break apart Zeal reaches into his pocket and pulls out a small wrapped packet that I recognise. It's one of the sweets from our last haul on Cornucopia, home of luxury goods and craftworkers. They are my favourite, an expensive treat; I thought they had all been used. Zeal sees the delight in my eyes and laughs. 'I thought it would be a delicious secret to keep, saved for just the right moment,' he says. 'And it was.'

'It's a bad trade,' I tell him, with a smile. 'I would have given you more than a hug.'

'You have given me more,' he says. 'A good gift of smooth pleasure in rough seas.'

He leaves me, stretching out the feeling between us, and I suck my sweet as I look out at Bounce's departure. It will come around again soon enough. I think and think, of things kept private and things saved for some future moment, of how we share and what we deny.

It gives me an idea.

I have traded with those like me, and those who had no point of connection beyond that moment. I have held out food and taken trinkets, the proffering for one thing for another, and I have accepted the satisfaction of that connection as the fulfilment of my kind. The satiation of different forms of desire to create a mutual understanding is my job, my life. My meaning. Love is, perhaps, the oldest trade. I love Zeal, but it is different to the way I loved Char.

I have negotiated lengthy contracts for technologies and bought land on hundreds of planets in exchange for our navigational maps and aids; where we have been before, and where we go next, matters to those who dream of escape so intensely that they cannot value the very soil they stand on.

I put on my suit, squeezing into the protective layer, then lower the helmet into place. Immediately everything is smaller, darker, contained. The suits were a trade made with a technologically advanced planet on the promise of payment later: WE OWE YOU are powerful words, motivating thoughts. Char struck that deal. It was the first of its kind, for bringers. The Artisan had gained a reputation for being a reliable ship, a superlative one. We can now trade on our own good name. Or we could, before the accident.

If I get the creatures of this planet to acknowledge me, what will they offer? The water they swim in? Their hopes and fears? Their love?

Any trade would be a triumph, and I want it, for myself. To be better than Tav and Zeal. I crave it like others have craved escape. This gulf between us has been growing since Tav's actions. I see it now.

I open the bottom seal in the belly of the Artisan, and lower myself into the water. Slipping out into the liquid of the deep is an anxious moment that quickly passes. The suit automatically makes all adjustments, somehow overcomes the intense pressure. It begins its own interior glow, spreading light around me. Here I am in my own world, my own head. A level of privacy, of individuality, I have not experienced in such a long time.

Business is the most personal thing in the universe.

Char and I traded between ourselves in love, for love. He gave me love and I took it, tended it, returned it ripened. An ever-growing investment.

Donn was our witness, and we paid him in time and laughter. He was our closest friend on board, and when the three of us were together it warmed us all. He validated us with his eyes and words, and in return we included him, cherished him. It is labour, to uphold love when you find it in others and do not have it yourself. What a kind, devoted one he was, wiser in the ways of trade. How I miss the way he would sit with us in the evenings, and we would listen as he told and retold his stories. That, too, was a venerable form of transaction.

It was a mistake. I hear Tav saying those words again and again.

No blame. Only sadness, shared equally, cut up and taken up. Worn as a heavy, heavy weight.

I'm approaching the hole.

Bounce will be here soon. This is a huge risk on my part. I am so small to such a creature, but I believe it will respond to me if I can make myself seen somehow – not as part of a ship, a cold craft, but as a living being. And the suit can shine as brightly as a star, make sounds to shatter all around it. Will it be enough? If it isn't, and Bounce does not see me, I might be crushed in its path.

But I want to trade, dispensing with that which I no longer want, and I swim hard, with purpose. The closer I get the more the hole scares me. It's massive. From the ship it looked – finite, somehow. The edges visible, the depth only hinted. But there is no end to it, no bottom. If it was to belch out its strange waves of force at this moment I would be shaken apart. But the waves are regular, and so is Bounce. Here it comes now, angling its body on the same invisible path it always takes. This is nothing like it seemed from the viewing room on the Artisan. Bounce is a monster. And I am in its way.

38

I turn on the lights and sounds of my suit, and I stretch out with my arms and legs, trying to make myself look larger. What does it want? What can I give it, and what will it give me?

Bounce is travelling fast. I can see nothing but its bulk; the suit's lights are blinding me. The feeling of its approach is in the water, in my bones. It does not alter. It does not see me or hear me. Too late to get out of the way, so I swim; I swim fast, faster, I feel it upon me, and I am buffeted and then caught in its wake, but I am not crushed, not hurt, not dragged into the hole. The suit stabilises me and I turn, and see it hit the spongy surface and flex upwards. Such joy.

Such joy. And then it swims on.

No trade.

I am halfway back to the Artisan before it occurs to me: did I close the seal behind me when I left?

I was anxious to slip away, to not have to justify my course of action to the others. Surely I wouldn't have forgotten that one crucial step in my haste. Surely.

The ship can keep a seal open at this depth for only a small amount of time, and I have no idea how long I've been gone. I am so tired; I can't make my body move any faster. But there's the alarm system. That's right. An alarm would sound before any damage came to the ship. The others will find the open seal, set it right. But there are other dangers. Anything could get in. Something we haven't seen before, haven't spotted since all our attention has been on the giants. A small, quick lifeform. A microscopic enemy. I am an idiot. I have opened us up to attack.

The water drags on my limbs. I have never felt so slow. What will I say to Tav, to Zeal? *It was a mistake.* Those are the only words that will come to me. If there is still a ship, if they are still alive, I will say them. And the ship comes into view. A shining dome in the light of my suit, and in the relief I find the energy for the final push back to the seal, which is closed and locked up tight, as it should be.

I punch in the code for outside access, and haul myself in. I remove my helmet and lie on the floor, breathing, just breathing.

I've done nothing wrong.

Why, then, do I feel so terrible?

Tav is beside me. She helps me sit up, she rubs my back. She begins the process of removing my suit, feeling for the joins at the back of the neck, on the wrists and ankles. For all her soft touch, I realise she is struggling with some strong emotion. Anger, maybe. 'I found the seal left open,' she says. 'One more minute and I would have put on a suit and come after you. You scared me. What were you trying to do? I can't lose anybody else.'

When I can speak, I say, 'Thank you. It was a...' I can't say those words, so instead I explain my theory. Trying to get the creatures' attention. It was not a stupid idea, I'm sure of it. I end by saying, 'I'm sorry.' Sorry for leaving the seal open. Sorry for losing my love and not having the strength to tell her how much I blame her for it. Sorry for everything.

She listens, then shakes her head, concentrates on the undoing of the suit, and says, 'No charge.'

A paradox:

To be unexpectedly freed from obligation only increases the sensation of owing it.

These are murky waters I don't understand. If we were being honest I would obviously be in debt to Tav. I would be making her meals, doing her favours. But I am not allowed to do these things because she has denied the obligation. Every time I so much as look in her direction I feel her reluctance, her fear that I might want her to face what happened.

No charge, she said. Negating the very basis of our lives.

I haven't dared to return to the water since, and we are running out of tricks. We tried warmth and music and imagery, maps and technology, but nothing attracts their attention. They are monoliths. They are stones upon which we might dash ourselves to bits.

Not long left.

It's lunchtime, and Zeal and Tav are playing tiles for treats.

They take it in turns to pull three tiles from the sack on the table. The tiles are engraved with shapes: squares, triangles, circles. Then they mix the six tiles together, remove and reveal one, and line up the remaining five. The trick is to guess which one will be found in the centre spot, trading information about what shapes remain. It takes more skill than a beginner might think, and I have never got the knack of it. I learned to resist the urge to play after losing more of my goods than I wanted to part with, including my pride.

Zeal is winning, as usual.

Tav plays enthusiastically in a currency she alone can offer: small poems, a few lines at most, scribbled on scraps of paper that she keeps just for this game. She seems to have hundreds of them in her head. I wouldn't mind knowing what she writes, but I never did win against her when I used to play, and they are for winners only, she says. That means she's really writing only for Zeal, and he reads each one with a smile turned inwards, folded neat at the corners.

He reads his latest win, smiles, and puts the slip of paper with the others. Then he starts to deal the tiles again.

'We're getting nowhere,' I say, surprising myself.

'Everything wants something,' says Zeal, in his good mood. It's another one of those familiar sayings. He's turning into an old bringer before my eyes.

'Maybe not. Maybe these creatures want for nothing. Maybe, right here, they have everything they ever wanted.'

'That's not the way the universe works,' says Tav, with exaggerated patience, as if talking to a child. Simply to needle her, I say, 'The dead want for nothing.'

They both look at me. Then they return their attention to the tiles, and play as if I am not there at all.

Only sadness, I remind myself. But the shares of sadness are not so fairly split.

I can see my own mistakes everywhere.

One error could lead to death, or destroy the ship. One misplaced comment can end the delicate balance between us all. How did we ever manage to go on, the three of us, after the deaths? I sit in the viewing room and run through what happened, over and over, while Zeal and Tav make final efforts to reach the giants.

Three last tries, they say. They have considered my idea and found it promising, and have taken to using the suits to head out together. *Three last tries and we'll give up. We'll go.*

It will be our first failure as bringers.

Our reputation will be ruined. The debt we owe will be called in, and we will have to sell the Artisan to pay. It's not the universe our people think it is. It does not work on trade alone, and there is no one principle that unites us.

The first try, with subsonic frequencies, comes to nothing. The giants do not acknowledge us.

I sit very still in the viewing room, and watch, and think of the past.

Char had a long-term relationship with the dry ones, who inhabit Sparse, a planet that would seem barren to any who do not know the ways to treat the land. He regularly offered them seeds for their underground gardens, and was paid in the sand-woven materials they made, which he favoured for trading elsewhere. *If we were ever to settle, just the two of us,* he once said to me, *I would become a weaver. I could make such patterns from this stuff.* But those were private words, filled with the kinds of fantasies he liked. He knew as well as I do that we are not the settling sort – that is the kind of trade that can never be struck well with the land for long – and he laughed as he talked of it.

On that final journey as five, Char took Donn with him and at the last moment Tav said, *Can I go too? I have an idea.* She had been dabbling in the arms trade, and had heard of a settlement deep in the desert who were looking for boundary weapons in order to protect against invasion. This was by no means likely, and it was not a concept they had come by themselves – other bringers had brought it to them, used it in order to sell them literature from the warlike tribes of Grasp, who spread their paranoia easily, enjoying its effect on others as justification for their own ways.

The sadness we felt at this development took away from our happiness, but it gave us a new opportunity, and Tav was determined to use it.

She packed equipment, and set out with Char and Donn. It seemed like any other trade.

The second try.

Tav and Zeal offer projections, beautiful, swirling, from the artists of Endeavour. The water distorts them, bends them into grotesque shapes, and the giants swim through them, untouched.

I see Tav swim faster, and imagine she is annoyed. I suspect she came up with the idea of offering Endeavour's goods, being a fan of them herself. Usually she is calm and methodical in her movements. I can picture how she looked setting up the boundary weapons around the village of dry ones on Sparse. She took the business of demonstrating products seriously. She told me later how Char and Donn played with the local children, swapping smiles and fun, learning the local pastime of kicking a hard circular ball into scoring zones. There would have been much running, much shouting, which is the only reason why I can imagine that Char and Donn did not respond to Tav's shouts to stay back when they kicked the ball too far.

No, no, get back, she said. She told me so.

When I ask her why she had loaded the boundary weapon for the demonstration, she said: *I wanted it to look good.* She does not trade in weapons any more. None of us do. Is that safer? I'm not sure. My imagination creates more weapons in the spaces between my knowledge; perhaps it would benefit one to know, to hold, the worst weapons being invented, and to control who can own them, rather than simply deny all responsibility. For there will always be weapons to trade, for trade's sake.

If everything can be traded, then everything is a weapon.

On the third try, I watch them take the strangest items from our stash out to the giants. There are some possessions that have yet to find a home. Ours contains games without rules, beans that don't grow, and dull rocks that get heavier if you squeeze them. They would be meaningful to someone, somewhere. Could this be their moment?

It was my idea to come to this unnamed planet and try the impossible. I thought it would be better than going on as we were. I think, perhaps, I wanted this failure even while persuading the others of the glory of success.

No, no, get back, Tav said, as loudly as she could, as loudly as she calls to the giants now, and they did not hear her for some reason, some reason we'll never know. The ball triggered the perimeter sensor, and the turrets trained on the moving targets in the zone. The system ascertained the targets would be most vulnerable to fire attack, and it burned seven of them to ash. Five of the dry children, and two members of the Artisan. Gone.

We had to pay a lot to the dry ones for the mistake. The good stuff. All the weapons, all the sweets, and more besides. Wait — not quite all the sweets, I remind myself, reliving Zeal's joy as he took the last one from his pocket to give to me. I remember the taste of it. A moment of pleasure that I had not expected, had thought to be impossible.

Defeated, Tav and Zeal return to the ship. Nothing good has come of this final effort.

We share a last meal before we are due to leave.

'An easy win,' muses Tav. 'That's what we need now. How about returning to Cornucopia?'

'It's not too far from here,' says Zeal. 'Good call.'

They don't ask me, but I offer an opinion anyway. 'Great,' I say, although I wonder what we will trade. I'm aware that I should voice my uncertainties. I'm selling them short with my acquiescence. Honesty is the first, best trade upon which all others are made, the old ones would say.

They go to their individual quarters to rest before we head off.

I return to the bottom of the ship, put on a skin, and head out into the water. I leave the seal open. I do it deliberately, and I do it without guilt. Only with sadness.

*

This is a game I've decided to play, the trick of the tiles. This is fate, some civilizations might say, but not bringers. I'm bargaining with the unknown, and I've never been good at such games. But since I've lost those I love I find I'm willing to risk more. Risk everything.

I swim to the hole, and wait there, as close as I dare to get, trying not to look into its darkness. How threatening it is to be dwarfed by something. It makes me wonder if the Artisan, our home, is a hulking mass to many. Do they trade with us because they are afraid of us? Do they think we would hurt them if they didn't agree?

Here it comes: the Artisan. The alarm must have sounded.

My first gamble has paid off.

It is approaching fast, lights blaring. It comes to a stop a short distance from the hole, and the lights dim. Then a small, intense beam separates from the body and bobs along, coming towards me. I need it to be Tav. She said she would come and find me; she has always been as good as her word before.

The movement of the body, the strong swimming style in the suit, tells me I'm right before she's close enough for me to see her face. I emerge from the hole and turn on the lights of my own suit. There's a surge of relief, strong, when she reaches me and starts talking. I can't hear what she says. I've kept the suit comms off, but even without it I catch her meaning perfectly. Angry pointing, harsh mouth. I would make the same expression if I thought one of us was placing the others in real danger.

And the anger – her anger – is what I want. We've tried everything but the feelings we try to keep out of all trades. Now I want them to bubble over, into the sea. Can the water amplify the emotions we feel? We've met creatures before that sense distress in others, and emotion is all we have left to trade in. Tav rages, all fury, and I add my own pain to the mix. I scream and thrash, and Bounce arrives. It comes closer.

It's working. I see it. It is altering its path to investigate.

It bears down on us.

I see Tav's eyes flick to its shape, widen. Her shout turns from anger to fear, and then Bounce is upon us, aiming right for us. I feel connection with its huge head, physical recoil, and I see its long mouth open and take in Tav. It swallows her whole. Then I am out of control, spinning through the water. The dark engulfs me, the hole takes me. I spin until my head can't take it any longer, and the dark sneaks into my suit, and steals me into unconsciousness.

Speed.

The sensation of speed, through the suit. I wake to find I am travelling fast, upwards, through the black. The pulsing waves that regularly emanate from the hole are driving me back out again, and I angle my body to surf them. Miraculous luck is on my side. I was pointing in the right direction. The suit withstands the intense pressure, and I shoot out of the hole to find myself back where I started, close to the Artisan, which is intact, and strong, and facing into the waves.

I should be dead.

I played the game, and I won. I won.

It is a trade, and we both leave victorious, Zeal and I. We triggered behaviour within them. We gave, and they took. And they gave us something in return too.

Personally, I have gained a sense of completion and understanding that is hard to put into words. I no longer feel unbalanced by sadness. Now my guilt matches it in ferocity.

With no body found, Zeal brought out all the little poems he had won from her, placed them in a bowl, and burned them. I will never get to read them now. *No blame. Only sadness.* We said those words together at the remembrance event, and I can tell he doesn't mean it. That's a feeling we now share equally, as crewmates should.

Apart from mealtimes, he avoids me. He is piloting the Artisan to Cornucopia, where we will trade the knowledge of how to reach the giants of the planet we have now named Outburst. It should pay off our debts and buy us something magnificent. Maybe another ship, so we can go our separate ways, find new crews with which to start over.

But as I look out over space, sitting in the viewing room, it comes to me that I will not leave Artisan, no matter what happens. I could live here alone. The knowledge of how to reach the giants is not the only thing Bounce gave me. It also gave me an understanding of how it can be better to hold everything inside, and not trade at all. I might try that for a while. I want to swim through this endless darkness, hiding in the blackest of holes, to banish all thoughts of who gives and who gets.

No blame. No sadness.

What do I have to trade for that?

The Emblem of Daydreams

Exercise equipment was set up around the yard for the benefit of all inmates. Only a few sessions in, it became obvious that some had stamped their ownership upon certain stations, not to be touched by others; the parallel bars belonged to the Emblem of Daydreams.

She stood between their straight lines, leaning on the bar closest to the fence with her back to the view of the rift.

Emblem had a theory about the rift. She suspected that, even glimpsed, it could keep one going with thoughts of escape. If the wire could be broken, the distance travelled, one could return to Earth: these were skills not beyond the inmates, perhaps, if they united against the guards. They did not unite. They were singular entities, could not be a collective. That was their nature.

How strange, Emblem thought, as she leaned and swayed on the parallel bars, *that they share the very trait that keeps them from collaborating.* She watched them observing the rift with their hungry eyes, and did not speak of her thought to anyone. She understood she belonged to the same paradox. The prisoner's dilemma: how can one trust when one is, essentially, untrustworthy?

She made a conscious, ongoing effort to ignore the rift. She had never looked at it directly, not even at the start of her incarceration, so long ago. She had a feeling that, if she focused upon it, she would see something she would not care to know. Instead, she pictured it as a golden horse galloping, coming towards her with its mane undulating in the breeze of optimism, stopping just behind her and waiting, waiting, for her to mount it and ride it home on an ecstasy of escape.

Many inmates milled in the centre, creating a loose circle. But The Emblem of Daydreams preferred to look at the others who had staked their claims to certain stations. The Song of Glad Service was performing a complicated move on the rings. It had impressive upper arm strength. The Expression of Simplicity was making a sculpture in papier-mâché at the art table. The treadmill turned for the many feet of the Hard Work Progressive. What a busy bunch.

The hour was approaching its end, and the masked guards began the process of persuading the inmates back into the penitentiary.

'*First Love* on the box in ten!' called the guard who preferred to walk the perimeter in an anti-clockwise parade. The thought of *First Love* was enough to start the process, for who could resist it? *First love*, thought Emblems, fondly. The concept touched her remit, but the show had little in common with human reality as she knew it. Still, she enjoyed its confections as much as the next inmate. She stretched out her wings, allowed them a brief shimmer, and Badge: To The Stars! stopped swivelling on his pommel horse to sigh at her beauty. He came to her, and held out a besuited, military arm, so she left her parallel bars behind and allowed him to escort her back indoors.

Nobody was a friend to anyone else, but Stars! had manners and bearing, and that attracted her greatly, like a moth to a light. They had ideological points in common, too, although he was obsessed with breaking free and entering the rift in a way she found unbecoming.

'I could aim no higher,' said Stars! as they waited their turn to pass through the gates, 'than to be by your side at this moment.'

'Romance is a pleasant pastime,' she said. 'But, you know, it is ultimately fruitless. Much like your own endeavours to escape. You are endlessly idling in your imagination, of which, naturally, I approve.'

He huffed. She liked to needle him, now and then. 'Shall I not come for you, then, madam, when I break free to the wide beyond?'

'Whenever you call, I shall answer,' she said, with a smile, enjoying the moment, knowing it would end in the recreation room when The Stars! would take his usual seat between High Morale Medallion and Chin of Integrity, and not give her a second thought until the next recreation period. How easily he could break her heart, if he chose to. She fantasised about the feeling of it, a little.

Alone was a good way to be. The solitary life was, in fact, essential for her well-being, although she had not imagined it would be enforced in a small cell at a time at the conclusion of her kind. They had been banished; well, it was probably for the best. She could not remember why.

She settled down on her plush velvet banquette, and *First Love* began.

Who had created this ongoing tale of entanglements and dalliances? Couplings and separations, every emotion lived on a frenzied plateau of self-obsession? Who were these actors? Sometimes the faces changed but the names remained the same. The other humans onscreen absorbed the alteration without blinking. How malleable, how capable of change, humanity was. She loved them and hated them for that, and she was entranced by the fact that Trez had developed feelings for Sherrie, but Sherrie was in love with Kamala, who was cheating on her with the gardener, Breck.

How quiet the recreation room was in the grip of *First Love*.

At the end of the episode, the box was switched off and the process of the packing away of the inmates began for the night. Each to their own place – Daydreams did not mind the plain white walls of her cell, viewless. She could cast her mind to amazing sights upon that bland interior. It was a more painful business for others, she knew, such as the Paddle Steamer of Patriotism and others of that kind, who had to be corralled nightly by the guards and negotiated down the corridor.

'Just a lake to claim,' muttered Patriotism, manoeuvring her bulk past Daydream's banquette. 'Just a body of water, I beg you, upon which the sun does not set.'

A stream of others, trailing in Patriotism's wake, were marched off, and the time was upon her. She stood, adjusted her skirts. She floated from the room, down the corridors, aware of the way the masked guards kept a respectful distance. She was powerful still, and they knew it. She had no idea how she had ever been subdued and brought to this place, but she was certain it had something to do with her reluctance to ever touch another human being again, or bestow her gifts upon them. What a waste it would be, to help them make leaps of the imagination. To take hold of those with smallness inside them and expand them, to blow hot thoughts into their delicate shells. It was a great love that had turned to icy hate inside her.

She entered her cell and heard the door click shut. Once the footsteps of the guards had receded, she cast pleasant, soothing vistas on the wall, keeping her mind far from the idea of escape:

A mound of gold from a ticket bought on a whim at a service station, under a rainbow, on a full moon, and being spotted from afar by someone powerful, your skill noticed, your potential spun to fame. And first love as it should be, yes, all shy looks and bursting hearts, and you are afraid to enter the room where they might be because you know you can't keep it from your features, but maybe you'll see it on their face too, imagine! What you might see on their face too. Trez and Sherrie do their best on that box, but nobody can fake that. There is a reality, and it is beyond this place. It is a golden horse to be ridden.

'The smallest of details are so important, aren't they?' said Disposable Trinket. She leaned in, nearly touching one of the parallel bars. It was, to Emblem, a serious imposition. 'Did you see the way Breck frowned, just a little bit, as he was watching the others through the window behind the chocolate fountain while they were having that charity fundraiser? Spoke volumes, didn't it?'

Since Trinket was so keen on the details, Emblem offered her a small grimace, to see if she would take the hint and push off.

Trinket took a step backward. 'I'm just saying, Breck's going to do something terrible. Wait and see.'

'That which is foretold is all the sweeter achieved,' said Emblem. 'Like time alone, say. The solitary life.'

'I'm unimportant, I know. But I have a right to exist! To stand here, by the parallel bars! To talk to the great and mighty car bonnet ornament!' It was a sudden bang of anger, loud and unexpected.

'How dare you?' said Emblem, unfurling her wings to full magnificence, and leaning forward on tiptoe. 'Are you looking for some kind of confrontation?'

'I just wanted to say how pretty the rift looks today, don't you think?'

'Don't play your petty tricks on me!'

'I'm all out. Spent. I have nothing else to offer,' said Trinket, loftily, taking a bow. As she straightened, she winked at Emblem, then sauntered away.

That whole thing had been a distraction, then. A mini explosion to draw the attention of the guards while – what? Who benefitted? And how come Trinket was doing another inmate's dirty work?

Emblem cast her eyes around the compound. She saw it. The space next to the pommel horse where Stars! should be: it was empty. That was his regular position of choice. Without his handsome posture the yard looked wrong to her. And nobody else was running to fill his gap. She locked eyes with The Monochrome Overcoat, who tweaked his mackintosh and jerked his head to one side; everyone was full of movement today. To his left, A Flower of Promise was humming, refusing to look at anything but their own roots. Strange behaviours. Flower lived to raise their head to the sky, the Rift, but they would not look up today.

The Rift called.

It was stronger than Emblem could remember feeling, that desire to see it, to let its reality overrun her fantasy. No, no. She couldn't become like the others. Her confidence in the separation that existed between them all – that, too, was missing. Banished by the absence of her infatuation, she closed her eyes, and tried to find her certainty.

When she opened them again, defeated, Stars! had returned.

He stood by the pommel horse in his wide stance, hands on hips, smiling. The earth around his feet was darker in colour, as if his very presence had changed the ground beneath him.

First Love:

Poor Breck, dumped by Kamala. His young heart forlorn and unravelled: *I'll never love again*, he says, and if he were a real person, if Emblem had a way to reach him, she would grant him idle thoughts of a better lover, a better life.

But then he gives a sideways glance to the waitress at the lower-class café he frequents. It's a new set to the show and she hasn't said a word of dialogue yet. All she's done is smile and pretend she knows her way around the Lavazza machine, but Disposable Trinket is right. It's all in the detail. *Where a door closes, a window opens*, thinks Emblem, and she spends the night picturing windows of all shapes and sizes, round, square, oval, opening on to chocolate fountains and open roads without a fence or a piece of exercise equipment in sight.

Balancing herself between the two parallel bars, Emblem wondered to herself: *Where does Stars! go?*

She pictured all sorts of solutions. An aura of invisibility, or a time machine. She considered that only her eyes misled her, during every exercise session. The silence of the others on the subject would seem to corroborate that theory, but those tiny movements they made gave them away.

No, it's not just me. He is gone, and then he returns.

Where does Stars! go?

He did not escort her any more. He did not come for her at the end of the exercise period, and he did not so much as glance in her direction. She wondered if he was afraid of what she might say to him. An act, like a jilted lover – did he not know that was not her style? Still, she felt wounded, deeply. She wanted him to know it.

First Love:

Ophelia lures Breck back to love.

She says: *It's not our choice to be free of the emotions of the world. The world entangles us. It wraps us up in its arms.*

They kiss, passionately, in the back room between the sacks of coffee beans. *I know this is sudden,* he gasps. *I will love you until the stars end. Marry me.*

But we have no money, she says. *No way to be together.*

I have money, says Breck. He reveals his secret identity. He is the millionaire son of Lord Lovington III, evil oil magnate, but he is determined not to inherit that dirty money. He has made his own fortune in futures while tending the privets. But now he will attempt to mend bridges. He will reach out to his family, from the bliss of his unexpected nuptials, and try to change the world for the better. Remake the world in wind and sunshine.

How will his grasping family take this?

Not well, guesses Emblem.

Ophelia is radiant as she walks down the aisle, but a troubling note sounds in the score. She's probably not going to last long.

Emblem wishes the business of details had never been pointed out to her.

When he finally did come to her bars again to offer his arm, she smiled, and took it serenely, as if she had never doubted his attentions.

'Lady,' he said, 'I delight in your beauty today, as I do every day.'

'Delighting from a distance is wise,' she observed, taking her time, pacing her walk. 'For when viewed closely, one can see faults so much more clearly.'

'But if the object is faultless, how much more worthy of admiration it seems when one holds it close. I must tell you...' He stopped walking, and patted her hand with a familiarity that riled and thrilled her, 'There comes a time when one must express a preference and stick to it: from a distance, or close enough to touch?'

'I don't see why one must decide, and never deviate.'

'Such moments come to us all.'

'Not to me,' she said, proudly.

He bowed to her, his eyes half-closed. Was that a glint of sadness? They walked on, to the gate, and he took his leave of her. She did not concentrate on *First Love* that evening, nor on her own thoughts. She imagined his hopes, his expectations, and what it must have been like for him on Earth, when he strived for ever better, ever farther, and asked humans to believe themselves capable of so much more.

The other inmates played their parts admirably in his escape. Emblem began to understand that she had been mistaken about their capacity for cooperation. They all had their own obsessions and squabbles, and yet Stars! had gifted some of his own courage to them when he told them of his plans. The more bravery he had bestowed on others, the more he had created in himself.

Emblem realised this in the moment the alarm sounded.

The masked guards raced out, flooded the exercise yard; she had no idea there had been so many, simply waiting in the wings for just such an emergency. It was a drama, everything a staged event, and Stars! owned the limelight with his absence. There were no gaps in the fence, no obvious means of escape. They searched and searched, then, in desperation, overturned the exercise equipment. Emblem clung to the parallel bars and refused to be moved, moaning at the sight of the trashed trampoline and the ripped-down rings. It took three guards to flip the pommel horse and find, underneath it, the tunnel. Dozens gathered, crowded around, peered in. There was a discussion. One guard was lowered into its depths – a tight fit, at the shoulders.

'Come on now,' said the guard at Emblem's side. 'Time to go in.'

She waited, wings unfurled.

Nobody emerged from the tunnel.

'Don't make me get physical,' said the guard by her ear, his voice quivering.

'I'm ready to return to the recreation room now,' she informed him, and floated to the gate, determined not to acknowledge the sounds of destruction and wonder around her.

If a guard went into the tunnel, it did not emerge.

For a long time, there was no exercise period. An additional episode of *First Love* took its place, and that kept most of the inmates calm, sated. Emblem fidgeted on her banquette as Ophelia revealed herself to be a terrible trap, laid for Breck. Barely human at all, with her mighty dedication to hurting him. Where was Ophelia's smallness, indecisiveness? Brushed aside, now it no longer served the plot. The series was ridiculous.

She stopped paying attention to the events onscreen and thought only of where the tunnel might lead. She knew she wasn't alone in this. Steamboat obsessed about it loudly – 'The hole might fill with water,' she often said as she sailed by. 'It leads to a lake, I know it, I know it. It will fill if we just watch. It's waiting to happen.'

Steamboat is right about one thing, thought Emblem. *Something is waiting to happen. It's in the tiny motions of my wings, and the way I turn my head from the screen, just a touch. Something is waiting to happen.*

First Love:

Breck: I can't believe you deserted me. You left my heart behind. You tore me to pieces, and laughed at what's left.

Ophelia: I was always destined for better things than you. And after the divorce your money will give me a way to prove it to the world!

Breck: How can you be so cruel?

Ophelia: You should try it some time.

Breck: You little….

He strangles Ophelia, and lays her dead body down on the ground.

Breck: What have I done? The love of my life. All gone. Everything good is gone.

When they were released back into the yard they found the equipment had been removed.

Everyone mingled in new, uncertain groups, except for Emblem. She marched to the spot where her bars had been and resolutely stood there, eyes averted from the rift. She stared back at the others, and at the tunnel.

It had been filled in, of course. Concreted over. The rumours, distributed mainly by a burstingly excitable Trinket, had been that it went all the way to the rift, and beyond. If that was true, Stars! might even have made it back to Earth. What was he doing there? Was he inspiring them to launch forth, to travel farther, rather than concentrate on what was close to them, part of them? To take such thoughts seriously, rather than see them for the daydreams they were?

She imagined him coming back for her, riding in on that beautiful horse she had pictured for so long. Or possibly battering down the fence in a reassuringly expensive car.

'Hop in,' he'd say.

'Breck!' she'd sigh. Wait – that was not the right name. Stars! did not have a real name; he was not human. But what did it matter, in her mind? She would call him Breck and she could be Ophelia, except things would never end between them. There would be no moving on to the next love, after the first.

She hated him for shaping her thoughts in this way. She was no longer separate, no longer alone, even though he had vanished. She was now part of this place, caught up in it. Controlled by it.

The others took turns poking at the tunnel.

There are better ways, she thought.

She closed her eyes and turned until she felt certain she was facing the outer fence, and beyond it, the rift. She bathed in its power, its glow, until she felt ready to look upon it.

It was a silver scar across the sky, surrounded by thunderhead clouds, a purplish cast to those towering masses. The rift gaped at its centre, as if whatever lay on the other side pushed against the seam for escape, revealing blackness. Movement. Many possibilities squirming, in which one could see declarations of first love, or the polished lid of a coffin. Expansion. Confrontation. Anything at all.

She leaned forward, poised on tiptoe, wings at the ready, then gave the smallest of jumps to take herself up. The fence was flimsy, pathetic. The air was rich; it lifted her with ecstatic ease. She did not look down. She fixed her eyes on the rift, steering towards its majesty, certain the clouds could not harm her. She would find her way back to humanity, to love, to the stars, to fantasies. To the kind of dreams she had once dared to give to others. She was the golden horse, riding to the rescue of all those who did not strive, but only dreamed of first love, final breath, beginnings and endings and escapes.

Your Hero

Barthon used his knowledge of the roads to outrun the chaos, found a clear stretch, and kept his foot down, watching the needle of the petrol gauge. All emotions lay outside the car. He had nothing, travelled light, without fear, guilt, shame. The wipers kept the grey ash at bay; it piled up, like feathers, like a pillow broken open. It formed an arc beyond the reach of the wipers. The air conditioning was efficient, bordering on icy.

This road was one of his favourites. It ran from west to east, across the hills, skirting a strip of forest between the cities and the sea. It dipped and rose with the contours of the land and was very straight. Barthon occasionally saw cars coming the other way, headlights on, and occasionally he overtook those travelling in his direction. Some swerved erratically, or were missing mirrors, bearing scrapes and dents. He was careful. The clock, set in the walnut dashboard, read 14:31.

He thought of his first car. It had been a Morris Ital in a shade of brown that nobody wanted, making it a bargain at auction. The engine had been old and thirsty, the clutch worn. All he'd known how to do before bidding was walk around it and kick the tyres, trying to look as if he knew what he was doing. He pictured himself from a distance, nervously counting out the twenty-pound notes; it was easy to remember the young man and the car with both affection and regret. He pushed that Ital hard, spinning doughnuts in the supermarket car park after the end of his shift, and overtaking on blind corners, escaping a tractor once by a hair's breadth, relying on the fast reflexes he had not appreciated. Then he had pulled over and breathed hard, hands shaking on the wheel, before starting the tired engine once more and creeping back home, meek, obeisant to the rules of the road for a change.

These were enjoyable memories, the fear eroded, the emotions faded.

One day the Ital's clutch, sick of teetering at the top of its biting point, had collapsed, leaving the pedal floppy under his foot, hitting the floor without resistance. It was beyond saving, at least, on his wage. He had cried when the salvage truck had taken it away. He was not ashamed, not very; wasn't it better to believe that all good things lasted forever, in some way? It was painful to find out he could not rely on them, and that had been his first real lesson.

The stretch of road ahead held the illusion of emptiness, but Barthon knew that its dips and rises could conceal hidden obstacles. He resisted the temptation to put his foot down to summon the boy he had been, and he was glad of the decision when a bumper came into view on his side of the road: a lone car, a Triumph Stag, at a stop, half on the grass verge, awkward on its thin wheels. The bonnet was propped open. A figure bent over the engine – a man in jeans, then Barthon was past, and he glanced in his rear-view mirror at the green Stag, a classic, and found himself indicating to pull over without giving it much thought.

He got out of the car, took a breath of warm, acrid air, and walked back to the man, who straightened, and revealed himself as a teenage boy with a dirty, frightened face. Maybe he was just old enough to drive. But he was big in the body, and fast, assuming a stance that might have come from an action film. 'Stay back,' he said, his voice not under control.

'It's okay. It's okay,' Barthon told him, holding up his hands. 'Can I help?'

The line of tension in the boy's shoulders relaxed. How easily he believed in good intentions. 'I need to get – do you know where…' His words petered out, and he stood there, staring at the car.

'Is it the engine? Beautiful cars, aren't they?'

'It's my brother's.'

Barthon didn't ask where the brother was. 'Shall I take a look?' he said, although he still didn't know much about engines. Still, it was what a man was meant to say.

The boy stepped back, and he took his place, checking the dipstick. It was immediately obvious to him that he could not mend it. He did all the things he could think of, just to keep the boy's fear at bay for a little longer.

There was nothing for it but to admit defeat. He said, 'I'll give you a lift. To a garage. You can get some help there, bring a mechanic back with you.'

'Yes, okay,' said the boy, much more quickly than he had been expecting. He shut the bonnet. It clanged, then clicked into place.

'Great,' he said, trying to inject a casual note into his voice, as if this was normal, a usual situation for him. He watched as the boy retrieved two large plastic bags – bags for life – from the back of the old Stag and locked the doors with care.

'My brother would kill me if anything happened to it,' the boy said, defensively.

Back in the Range Rover, soft jazz sweeping from the rear speakers, they swapped names. Liam was keen to talk. He wasn't far from home at all, he said, but his village had been close to the sites, and had been one of the first to be declared unsustainable when the earthquakes started. They – he didn't define who he meant by that – had left for his uncle's, on the coast, not thinking much about the sea level warnings until they came to a river with burst banks, pouring over the way, sweeping up cars as it went. Turning back, they'd made it to higher ground, tried to get a room in a hotel without success. Liam's words dried up as quickly as they'd started, and Barthon did not want to ask questions about the gap between the then and the now. The missing hours, the unaccounted-for people.

Instead, he said, 'This road is so quiet. I haven't seen many people at all. The motorways are a nightmare.' It was a phrase one might say in usual circumstances.

'It's weird,' said Liam.

'I don't know,' he said, his mind working, 'I can think of reasons. It was made pretty much obsolete when the dual carriageway went in.' He felt very calm. Maybe it was the influence of having a passenger again, as he was meant to for this journey. 'You can choose the music. We don't have to listen to this stuff, although there's no radio, of course. I have some CDs in the glove box. I'm old school, I'm afraid.'

'I like this,' said Liam. 'It's like – being in a film.'

'The two cool adventurers drive off into the sunset,' Barthon said, and laughed.

'Or one of those commercials. These seats are so comfy. I could fall asleep.'

'Leather, heated.'

'Beautiful,' Liam said.

It triggered a memory for Barthon, not through similarity, but because of difference. He tried to push the thought away, but it was too late; there was Ben, in his mind, wearing that unimpressed expression that always annoyed him so. *It's a fucking ugly, wasteful monster, Dad, and it should be banned. I'll take the train.* He was like Tanya in his chin, the line of it, mother and son both pitiless when they disapproved of his choices, but at least Tanya would let it drop, had found ways to forgive. A trick Ben had not learned yet. Was that youth? Perhaps one had to learn forgiveness, or be asked to supply it, many times over, before finally giving in. Tanya had come to it in good grace, eventually, forgiving him for many things. But she would not forgive him for this latest disappointment, he already knew.

'I have a thermos of coffee and some cookies on the back seat,' he said. 'A bag of stuff, actually. Help yourself.'

Liam reached back, craning his body into the space between them to find the plastic carrier that held the supplies. Rustling: then a return to his seat, a cookie already in his mouth.

'Hungry, huh?'

'Mmm.' Quick bites later, the cookie was gone. 'Yeah, really hungry.' He had the thermos between his knees; he unscrewed it, loosened the inner seal, poured out the coffee. The car's suspension was more than up to the task of keeping an even keel, but Barthon slowed a little anyway, to ensure no spills. Smooth, onward rolling. On the other side of the road there had been a crash. Three cars lay abandoned, smashed together in impact, glass and silver scattered: two saloons and a cabriolet. They had been moved to the verge. It was not a new event. Barthon wondered where the people were now. Had they walked free, without a scratch on them? Modern engineering was a marvel.

'My son works in the northeast,' he said. 'He's an administrator for a geological surveyor. You working?'

'I'm doing an apprenticeship with a builder. We were on a new estate, and it got sinkholed. The whole thing.' Liam was excited by it, Barthon realised. He described coming to work, finding it gone, and he threw out his arms as he said, 'It was massive, just this massive hole.'

'Lucky it happened overnight.'

'Yeah.'

'A near miss.'

'So your son's in the north east?'

'Yep,' said Barthon.

He could feel the ramifications of that sink into the boy, and it ended the conversation. Tanya had said, *But his office was on a hill, it was raised, he has a chance, you have to try to get to him. Take supplies.*

The memory triggered the urge to check his phone. Relief followed – there was no need to see if she had tried to contact him, or to explain why he had given up, turned around. The mobile networks were down. He preferred the phone this way: silent.

If he had reached his destination, found Ben, driven up and said, *I'm here for you, I'll take you home,* would his son have swallowed his principles and climbed into the car? Would he have smiled, thanked him, all gratitude, and accepted its protection?

I'll take the train.

But the lines are all gone, he would have replied. *All the lines are gone.*

Barthon nudged up the volume of the jazz.

A service station came into view. It was a small one, with a café beside it, and the signs for them both were chunky, bright emblems, designed to catch attention.

'There,' said Liam.

Barthon indicated and slowed. He checked the mirror, pulled into the slip road, completing the smooth actions even though he could see immediately that everything was closed. Not only that: broken. The pumps dry, the hoses snaking along the forecourt, and the windows of the station and the café smashed. All the shiny delights were wrecked. He didn't bring the car to a halt, but drove carefully around, avoiding the worst of the detritus, and pulled back on to the road. He sped up to that comfortable speed, to the point before the car's whisper became a growl.

'We'll try the next one,' he said.

Liam said, 'How much petrol have you got?'

His eyes flicked to the unmoved needle. 'You don't need to worry. The tank is huge. And these cars are surprisingly economical. People don't believe it, but they are.'

The boy relaxed back into the leather seat. Then he said, 'Can I have something else to eat?'

'Help yourself. There's loads of it. I thought I'd bring everything. I didn't know what Ben would want –'

'Your son?'

'I was meant to be picking him up.' Barthon felt the familiar tension return to his shoulders, from hours of driving, and the tightness in his foot, resting on the clutch. He should have got an automatic after all. Regular driving had created issues of the body, from years on the road. He'd started as a medical representative, eating up the miles in his Renault, hopping from surgery to surgery, before giving it up for a desk job just before the first lockdown. Good timing, really. He'd taken to working from home. The view from his study window, over his garden with the stretch of lawn down to the gravelled path and the little fountain Tanya loved, permanently trickling just a little water into its bowl over balanced pebbles. 'I couldn't get through. I'll try again later.'

'You going home, now?' Liam had found the muffins, was unwrapping the plastic.

'No. I mean, yes, but I thought I'd go up to this spot I know first, with a view out over the hills. Just for a change of scenery. You can see the whole county. I used to eat my lunch in a lay-by up there, when I was a rep. Years ago, this was.'

'Is it far?'

'No no.'

Barthon became aware of the boy's misgivings: a sudden wariness in the way he sat. Maybe it sprang from being fed and watered. Once those basic issues of survival were taken care of, concerns about the future could sneak in again. 'It's not a fixed plan,' he said. 'I don't think anyone's got fixed plans any more.'

'Shame,' said Liam.

'Ha, yeah, shame,' Barthon echoed, thinking it a joke, but he heard a repressed noise, half a hiccup, and caught the shaking of the boy's shoulders in his peripheral vision, and remembered how young he had once been himself, and how emotions could not be controlled at that age.

Then he remembered Ben, walking down the drive, laden with bags. *I'll take the train.*

If the Range Rover had taken him through the traffic, around the fires and fault lines, the panic, the fast collapse of the land – if he had reached Ben's office and found it still standing, and Ben within – what would his son have said? Would he have stood his ground, and refused to get into the monster? Or would he have sat there, in the passenger seat, with gratitude, and cried his own tears for his own reasons?

The jazz CD ended. It took only a minute, maybe two, for the silence to become oppressive. Barthon felt such relief when Liam flicked open the glovebox and selected a disc, classical this time. Operatic arias. He ejected the jazz, and pushed the new disc into the player.

'Good choice,' Barthon said, over the opening bars. Opera lasted for hours; it could feel never-ending. It might even get him all the way to the beauty spot he was aiming for.

They passed a battered old sign. A stack of suitcases was stacked against it, and a wooden chair, tipped on its side.

The sign read:

Next services: 27 miles.

'We'll make that in no time,' he told Liam. 'There's a recline switch on the left side of the seat, if you want to get some rest.'

Fed, watered, now offered sleep: this boy, at least, was safe. Liam tilted the seat back, not far, as the singer poured out his heart and the players made their music.

He had bought this CD on an impulse, spotting it in a service station amid racks of snacks and newspapers. Which journey had that been? Picking up Tanya after a trip to a spa retreat, he recalled. She'd gone for a week, somewhere west. Not this car, but the one before, that got rear-ended and written off a few months later. It hadn't been a serious accident, but it had helped him to persuade Tanya to go for this bigger, safer, model. Better visibility. He was high up, protected.

The ash was falling faster now, and an acrid smell had managed to penetrate the air conditioning. The sky was lost to the thick flakes. Visibility was definitely worsening, but he could make out enough to keep going with the wipers on full. Close by, something must have happened, just as it had in the north-east. Perhaps he was no longer driving away from the worst of it. No, that couldn't be right. The road was very straight; he knew where it went. He had found its unblemished line, reliant on the accumulated knowledge of back routes and little-known throughways. She had said, *If anyone can find a way through, you can. You bought this car because you said it could get through anything.* Four by four. Traction control. The next soprano had an amazing voice, he had always admired it, bright and cold and clear through the thousand-pound speakers.

He almost missed the turn for the service station.

The familiar sign poked through the grey at the last moment; he swerved, slammed his foot on the brake, and felt the seatbelt cut across his chest to keep him in place. The ABS did its job, and control was not lost. Liam woke, of course. That was a shame. The boy put his hands to the dashboard and said, 'What's happening?'

'Sorry,' said Barthon. 'I nearly missed the turn. My fault. I was daydreaming.' He drove the car up to a pump, checked the central cubbyhole for his wallet, then saw the yellow marker clipped in place:

sold out

please try

another pump

He pulled forward, and found the same marker. The lights of the station were off. He knew he should get out of the car and check around, maybe try to get into the service area.

He said, 'Damn,' but mildly, so as not to alarm the boy. He left the car idling.

'Is there anyone here?' Liam said, craning forward, trying to see through the ash.

'I don't think so.'

'What should I do? Should I get out here and wait? I need to get back to the car. It's my brother's car.'

'It's up to you, of course, happy to let you out, but I don't think you'll find any help here. You've come a bit of a distance now. Too far to walk back.'

'Yeah.'

'We can go on,' Barthon suggested. 'You might have more luck at the next stop.'

Liam's hand was on the door release. 'Is there enough petrol for that?'

'The tank's huge.'

'Is it?'

'These cars are famous for it.' Barthon watched as Liam put his hands back in his lap. He gave him a moment more, to be sure. 'Ready to get going again?'

The boy nodded.

He edged the car forward, swung around the curve behind the station, and returned to the road. The ash had lifted, a little, he thought. Visibility was improving again. The needle still hadn't moved.

He had a theory that it was not running on petrol any more. That it had reached a point of endless, eternal running, doing exactly what was needed of it. He was so glad he had bought it. An investment, not a luxury. It held him, supported him, understood its role.

He did not tell the boy this. He continued to follow the road, listening to the music, thinking of nothing much but how his hands felt on the padded wheel.

Wrapped

Part One

12 April, 1919

No great evil has befallen any of us yet. I suppose it is only a matter of time until an accident lays low one of the workers, or my skirts tangle in a rope and trip me up, or a sandstorm descends. Then Khefatra will receive the blame.

Khefatra. Her mask is a frightening sight to behold. The first guides panicked and ran from the burial chamber when we first opened the outer sarcophagus, but even back in the relative safety of my tent I can understand how our workers believe she holds a curse; to simply look upon the bronze head that bears her carved visage is to feel queasy. Is it an accurate depiction of her, or does it represent the feelings of those who served her? That open, contorted mouth, and the thick wrinkles around the eyes and nose are unlike anything I have seen. The masks of the dead are meant to be serene in their countenance; this is a figure disturbed, and disturbing.

I wish I could have known her.

I have spent my life in pursuit of her, and I maintain my theory that she was a ruler of her people. A forgotten Pharaoh, the first clue to her importance to be found in the fact that her name had been scratched through in so many records: what did she do to deserve such a fate? Only painstaking research, the piecing together of clues that others have attempted to destroy, led me to suspect that her burial chamber remained intact, to be found under the sand in an area that fell back under the control of the ancient Libyans shortly after her death. And so my dear

Nigel arranged funding and permissions, and here we are, at the culmination of my great undertaking.

Culmination? Hardly. As I write I realise that the word is inappropriate. Yes, I have found her chamber. I have already documented what has been found within: the ushabti containing the dust that is all that now remains of her vital organs; the small clay boats with linen sails that lasted no more than an hour in the desert air before disintegrating. But this is only the beginning of my work. Now I must hunt, and translate, and find irrefutable evidence of her reign, and of what befell her. This will finally satisfy my curiosity, and also secure my place amongst the works of those who have long inspired me: Carter, Maspero, and my own father.

Tonight, as my dependable Waleed pulled me back up from the chamber, hefting upon the rope attached to the canvas sling which has become my vehicle to Khefatra's remains, I found Nigel waiting for me by the mouth of the hole to offer me tea. I told him he was a marvel, and he replied with a warm smile that I, in fact, was the marvellous one. His admiration for my skills as an archaeologist and researcher has long been one of the greatest blessings of my life. I remember when he first proposed, at Kew, under a potted palm, and he said I was a true original. I asked him, then, if he felt he could support me in my endeavours rather than seek to control or curtail them.

'Ursula Templeton,' he said to me then, in words that will stay with me forever, 'You are unique. Your work is as important to me as it is to you. It must continue. I will make certain that it does.'

I chose my husband wisely. Even if he does snore, rather: a sound that is currently assailing me as I write, sitting across the tent from the bed at the small travelling desk that accompanies me on all of my travels.

Snoring is a small price to pay for a man who understands me so. I never thought to find one. I am out of my time, and therefore must select allies carefully who will make sure I am not imprisoned in the strictures that society sets upon us.

We are a pair, Nigel and I. I provide the knowledge and the money (one must remain forever grateful for father's work, and the inheritance it provided) and Nigel greases the wheels of the world with his charm. How could the Libyan government refuse his requests? I know I could not.

15 April

At the end of this long and terrible day I wish to write only one word.

Enough.

But this journal is for posterity, not for my own whim. So I must record the fact that Khefatra is no longer mine alone. She is to be taken from me under the guise of practicality when, in fact, the two arguments made contradict each other:

That this is a find of no real significance.

That the find should be in the care of the British government's chosen representative alone in order to ensure proper handling and classification.

So which is it? Does this uncovered chamber not matter at all, or is it of such importance that a mere woman cannot handle the task of exposing it? It is the very hypocrisy that lies at the heart of so many men; they want everything their own way, and when I point out the failings in their logic I am told that I am simply not intelligent enough to understand it. They speak their private language of power, and I am not afraid to point out that it is often gibberish.

Doctor Morrowley arrived just before the sun had unleashed its midday heat, with a large caravan of workers in tow. Luckily, we were prepared for him. The camels kicked up a cloud of sand that Waleed had spotted on the horizon, so we were able to hide some of the smaller pieces within our tent – but moving the sarcophagus itself was out of the question. So, with the greatest of reluctance, I left Khefatra in her resting place and emerged to greet the Doctor directly.

I have already recorded my thoughts on the theories and practices of Doctor Morrowley. I will not repeat them here except to illustrate them with today's example of his failure to comprehend the significance of my find. He insisted upon entering the chamber without my presence and when he emerged, heaved back into the now sweltering sunlight by a team of his own workers, he immediately took out a notebook and pen and began to list the artefacts he had spotted within. I stood behind him and watched, over his shoulder, as he wrote his inventory. All he had seen by the light of his lamp was what could be taken – not what should be cherished.

His attention was, of course, fixed on the great death mask. I could tell from the way his hand shook as he wrote of it that he knew it was a miraculous find.

The sarcophagus itself, he listed as such:

Casing (engraved with symbols) that contains a wrapped figure.

I need write no more.

I tapped his shoulder and waited for him to put away his notebook and pen before informing him of who she was, and how I had come across her resting place through my arduous study of many years. He replied that he had no time for 'emotional theories' and would look to ascertain the identity of the corpse after crating it and moving it to the Egyptian Antiquities Museum, as already agreed between the two governments.

At that point I will admit I abandoned any pretence of civility. I begged him not to treat her in such a fashion, and he called for smelling salts so I should not be 'overcome by hysteria'.

Ever faithful Waleed then escorted me back to my tent while Nigel attempted to reason with the man. I sit here awaiting the outcome of their negotiations; I can hear them speaking in their reasonable tones. I already know I cannot bear to lose the one thing Morrowley will demand. He leaves me with no choice.

17 April

I have done something so profoundly antithetical to my nature that I cannot quite believe it. I feel weakened by my own actions; I can no longer claim strength through my moral impregnability.

I am on a ship, bound for London.

Money changed hands to arrange my transport at such short notice; I did not see how much. And then I bade goodbye to Waleed. We parted dockside, and he must run. He will be blamed and hunted for my actions until such time as I can clear his name, and I will owe him a great debt forever more that I cannot hope to pay.

I am both a thief, and a desecrator of the one thing I have always purported to love.

If there had been any way to take Khefatra's body with me, I would have done so. But how could I possibly move her? I am but one woman, travelling alone, and that in itself draws suspicious eyes. To then commandeer enough porters to move a crate big enough to contain her – no. Besides, I could not have brought her up from the darkness. I will leave that to Morrowley. No doubt he has already done so, if he has not decided to pursue the mask himself.

I must hope that he has swallowed the story we concocted. I will not know if this has worked until Nigel writes to me. Will a letter from him beat me back to England? Perhaps, if it travels on one of the newer, faster ships. My own journey must take at least a week, with a stopover in Lisbon. I must be patient. I can use this time to make my observations about the mask, which currently sits within my trunk beside me here in this cabin. I heard the porters complain of the weight after they had delivered it to me: 'Women and their baggage!' Such common assumptions about my affection for material possessions over knowledge will allow me to hide in plain sight, so I shall not take offence this time.

And now to work. I shall immerse myself in the mask to make the time pass, and my doubts shall disperse. I am the same as I always was! Yes. I will stay the same. Work will make me so.

18ᵗʰ April

Looking back over these pages, I realise I will have to record my recent actions more fully. I cannot escape them, and I will not justify them: that would be an act of moral cowardice. I can only write down what happened and hope to find some future understanding within it.

On the night following the arrival of Doctor Morrowley to the excavation site, my mind would not be stilled. As I lay beside my gently snoring Nigel, I noted how my breath erupted from my mouth in plumes, and then dispersed in the cold tent. In, out, in out: breathing, the act of survival to which we are all bound. Khefatra did not breathe any more; she had no care for the worries of this world. I almost envied her.

Then I heard a voice. It was, unmistakeably, the voice of my mother, close to my left ear, as if she crouched beside the bed, her mouth by my pillow.

We will only be given what we can each bear to carry.

I do not think of my mother often. She was an uneventful woman who eschewed meaningful conversation for endless platitudes, and I soon learned to cease listening when she spoke to me. From quite a young age I craved only the company of my father, and awaited his return from his latest expedition so he could tell me stories of his adventures throughout the dark continent. What a mark he made upon the world. A mighty river bears his name proudly – as did I until my marriage. In a curious way I was glad to leave the surname of Templeton behind and step out from his long shadow to begin my own adventures as Mrs Ursula Carleton. Although he had been dead for many years before my wedding, I still felt his presence and even thought to hear his strong, deep voice at times.

Why, then, would it be my mother who whispered to me?

I can think of no reason. We did not grow closer after his death. She had not been strong to start with, and his absence seemed to diminish her further. Her only interest became the regular visits of friends, colleagues and followers of my father who asked to stand in his office and leaf through his numerous diaries. She would invite them to stay to tea, and then regale them with his stories, mixed with a heavy dose of her own moral idioms, which embarrassed me greatly.

She died quietly three years ago, slipping away in her sleep: an end that suited her. I have not missed her sayings from that day to this.

We will only be given what we can each bear to carry.

It was, indeed, a phrase she might say. Meaningless when examined closely, except... except this time I understood. It was a veiled command of a kind my mother would never have dared to utter. Did I misunderstand her throughout my life, or had some creature taken her voice and used it to propel me forward? All I can write is that I felt certain that I needed to rise, to dress, and to slip from the tent to step between the sleeping workers on the sand until I found Waleed, roused him, and bade him to lower me into the chamber.

Darkness is darkness; it is not possible to find a colour beyond the utter black that dominates where the sun's rays no longer penetrate, and yet somehow the burial chamber, that night, seemed blacker than ever before. I clutched the handle of my lamp and thrust it before me, but it could not banish the fear that I felt. The eyes of the Gods were upon me from where they had been painted on the walls so many years ago: Horus, Heqet, Thoth and Anubis watched me fumble my way to the sarcophagus, clumsy in terror, and reach out for the death mask of Khefatra.

I knew it would be heavy, but I soon found there was no method by which I could carry both the mask and the lamp. Eventually I gathered all my courage, and abandoned the lamp, leaving the warm circle of its light as I edged back to the sling with the mask filling my arms, its grotesque features turned up to mine.

With the last of my strength I managed to position the mask within the sling; Waleed then hauled on the rope. Up went the great treasure, and there followed minutes of agonising silence before the sling descended once more. Silence? Not quite. I must be honest. I thought I heard my mother's voice again, faintly, emanating from the far wall that bore the painting of Heqet.

Bear to carry

An echo, perhaps? I imagined her retreating, sinking back into the wall, turning away from me, and I found within me an intense desire to chase her and ask her, just this once, to speak plainly. I think I would have done so, but for the lowering at that moment of the sling once more. Waleed called my name, once, with urgency, and I positioned myself within so he could pull me up from the chamber.

When I returned to the tent, Nigel was awake and nearly dressed, putting on his boots to come in search of me. I explained my plan: to abscond with the mask and complete the examination of it within my own time, to then better repudiate Morrowley's half-baked theories.

'Bold,' he said. 'Too bold.' I wondered then if I had finally asked too much of him. Then he smiled, and said, 'It's worthy of a man. You never will accept less than that, will you?'

I said, 'Never,' and kissed him.

He then honed the details, persuading me that it would make sense for him to stay behind and blame a worker for the theft of the mask, then offer to work alongside Morrowley, thereby keeping our enemy close. My own sudden absence could then be explained as a resurgence of a hysterical issue needing the care of my personal physician. No gentleman could question such an occurrence.

I miss Nigel terribly already – and Waleed, also. My right hand man. Poor Waleed. But he assured me he can hide away and remain free until the truth can be told. How brave he is. I must do honour to his sacrifice by working hard to find my answers from the mask. Let this task commence immediately!

22nd April

Over dinner Captain Braylock enquired after my health. I thanked him for his concern and attempted to eat a little more of my lamb chop, which was on the fatty side. Just writing of it now makes my stomach clench; I abandoned it when I could stand no more, and was aware of his puzzlement as I hurried from the table.

I had hoped that claiming mal-de-mer would allow me to be left in my own devices within my cabin in the main, which is small but adequate for my needs. In truth, I have felt terribly nauseous; the sea is rough, and the sky is so very overcast and gloomy whenever I venture out on deck. But it is not only the weather than unsettles me so. It is the mask, and the messages it contains within.

Of course I was expecting to find carvings on the interior of the mask. That could hardly come as a surprise to any self-respecting Egyptologist. But just as the visage is unusual, possibly unique, so the Hieratic used within conveys a message unlike anything I have seen.

The symbols are tiny and they are numerous. Every inch of the interior surface is covered, and in places there is even overlapping to the point of unintelligibility – how could anyone translate these scorings in entirety, ranging from deep gashes to the lightest of pressures, made in a hand that ranges from violent outbursts to the tenderest of care?

Do I really believe that this is the work of one writer? I do. There are clear similarities in the strokes; a voice reaches through the dark centuries, shouting, whispering, begging me to understand.

A day's work revealed one small phrase to me. One phrase, from so many, carved above the right eye socket, and the act of translation revealed more than the words themselves. It

79

connected me once more to that eerie occurrence on the night of the theft, in a way that I cannot begin to comprehend:

Tears and smiles can come together

This is the exact phrase my mother often said to those who visited the house after the death of my father. A weak platitude that was one of her personal favourites, she bored me incessantly with it. I have checked my translation many times over.

I hear both my mother's voice and an older, wiser presence when I read these markings. Which is to be believed? Or am I simply imagining both? I must press on.

Sea air, it seems, is not conducive to a clear head after all.

24th April

It's not the air that is to blame at all. It is my own body. To create life whilst I was in the midst of studying an ancient, long-dead world… I have always looked only to the past, and now I must look forward instead.

I cannot begin to record how I feel about this event because I simply do not know myself. I veer wildly from excitement to despair, which shames me. Surely I should be delight itself with such news? Is this not what a woman is made for?

And yet the truth is I have never quite been that woman.

I will write Nigel a letter telling him of our news as soon as I return home. I wish I could see the pride in his eyes as he learns of our news, and allow that pride to infect me. But the thought of it will be enough. Yes, I can be happy at Nigel's joy.

Captain Braylock insisted upon the doctor conducting an examination for my sea sickness, and I am now glad that he did so even though at the time I was filled with irritation, and protested. 'You must be taken care of,' he said. I loathe such sentiments but perhaps, this time, he was right. The doctor enquired after certain private issues and then told me of the baby.

The baby.

He is a young man with a charming yet professional manner, and he tells me I am at least three months along! I simply did not consider it. I lost track of all time in the desert; besides that, I had never had a concern for such issues. Well, now I must begin to do so. I do not think I would have noticed my condition for some months to come; I am so unobservant about such matters.

26ᵗʰ April

It transpires that it is extremely difficult to sit around like a Bakewell pudding and think of nothing but the welfare of one's internal passenger.

During the stopover at Lisbon yesterday the Coddings (a dear old couple celebrating their anniversary) insisted upon keeping me company on board while others disembarked to see the castle. It was deemed for too adventurous for me; I learned of this from Mrs Codding, who informed me in a low voice that everyone had been told of my condition to ensure that I am taken care of properly at all times.

We played nothing but three-handed cribbage for hours – hours that I could have spent working.

But I must confess, I continue to work when I cannot be monitored by others. I hate to tell untruths to such well-meaning souls as the Coddings, but what they do not know cannot hurt them. So, while crew and passengers sleep, I work as if my life depends upon it. I simply cannot change my nature – and, what's more, I have come to the conclusion that to do so would be detrimental to my health and therefore also to the health of my baby. I know Nigel would agree with me on this matter.

Onwards. I made progress last night, and think I will have translated the long phrase over the left eye by dawn tomorrow.

27ᵗʰ April

It cannot be right.

I must start again. I mistranslate – no. It would be better to start again.

She glowers at me so. She whispers in my mother's voice. I am disappointing her.

28th April

Damn them all! Why can they not give me a moment to myself? I cannot think with the Coddings forever hovering outside my cabin door.

I will be so glad to see Southampton; there will be transport awaiting me for Sussex, and once I am within the four walls of my library I will be able to concentrate on what has occurred.

But there is no doubt that I cannot do good work here, and I am making terrible errors: errors in translation, and in judgement.

I will return the mask to my trunk, and try to remain calm until I can unpack it in peace.

1st May

I only think of her expression. That terrible grimace. Why? Why, combined with such words? She haunts me.

The steward has just knocked on the door; we have docked. Disembarkation is commencing.

The curse comes for me. I do not feel well. I fear for my thoughts. I fear for my child: what is within me? I fear it is she. Surely it is she.

Part Two

September 20th

The mask is deciphered, and I am myself again.

I am uncomfortable for much of the time. I have grown so large, and will become larger still, but I find my mind has a clarity once more that it has lacked for many months. I feel an optimism for the new task awaiting me: motherhood. I wish to excel at it – to raise a person of character who will make their own mark upon the world. Yes, now I have ensured the remembrance of Khefatra, and my own undeniable abilities as an Egyptologist, explorer and translator, I will look less to the past and give my all to the future instead.

It is good to write of my personal thoughts once more. I did not dare, for a while. Not while Doctor Sanding – an old friend of Nigel's – watched me so closely, looking for signs of increased agitation, for I am certain he would have insisted upon reading every word within this journal if he had known of it. I hid it away and worked only upon my translation in the hours they allotted to me. Thank goodness for Nigel's intervention by letter – it was only his insistence that refusing to allow me to work would exacerbate my unrest that persuaded the good doctor to allocate me two hours of time in my library every day.

On the subject of letters: I wrote to Nigel this morning and included the first translation of the Hieratic with instructions for him to pass it to Morrowley, and reveal that the mask is safe and within our possession. This is my bargaining chip; I know Nigel will play it wisely. The translation itself is a most enlightening and informative document. I will admit only here that I have taken the liberty of omitting the sections that reminded me of my mother's advice. Although I dreaded finding more such snippets, in fact I found only two – one above each eye socket – and I have decided that it was only my ever-busy brain at work, making vague connections that later came to be obvious. For it is true, although I could never have rationally foreseen it, that both my mother and Khefatra were supplanted and diminished. Belittled by their own choices. By the very men they loved.

I have come to realise that my mother would have been quite a different woman without the influence of my father upon her. He was always the centre of our lives, and he enjoyed that position immensely. But I now understand that becoming a satellite to another extols a high price. It sucks the colour and vivacity from one's being. I, for instance, could not even begin to reach my potential until I had moved from my father's sphere of influence. In the case of my mother, she lost sense of who she was if she was not part of him. I did not know her at all; the person I knew was only part of the shadow cast by my father: she became nothing more than a living ghost of the girl she had been.

But what of Khefatra? How could a Pharaoh have been but a ghost?

The mask gave me my long-sought answers. It is clear that she was one of the children of Ptolemy XII. Upon his death she acceded to the rule of Egypt, and she commanded the might and wealth of that nation for six years, alone, which is a magnificent achievement. The usual path was for a female ruler to be married to a male sibling to consolidate power, but the scribe of the mask is definite that no such union happened. In fact, the deaths of her siblings is recorded – the cause of death? I can only speculate.

There then followed a period of prosperity, described as 'blessings from Heqet'. Heqet was the goddess of fertility and childbirth; did Khefatra give birth, then? Have many children of her own, without a husband? What an astonishing thought.

At that point, the mask records, Khefatra appointed a chief consort. She did not take a husband; the scribe is clear on this point. But powers are given to the consort, who is highly favoured. Perhaps she loves him. He grows stronger, even as Khefatra begins to weaken. 'Heqet withdraws her gifts': that is how this weakness is described. I hazard a guess that Khefatra's fertility has ended – through illness, or through natural changes in the body? There are so many aspects to her life that we will never uncover.

The consort moves against her. He seizes power for himself.

She is taken away. If she did have children before he became her chosen partner, they were removed too. Probably murdered. Not even their names remain.

The consort becomes ruler supreme. He takes the name Ptolemy XIII and he erases as much information as he can that might reveal he is not a rightful king. He obliterates written records of Khefatra wherever he finds them, and has dates changed to show that he was the natural successor and child of Ptolemy XII.

She is, at least, granted a proper Egyptian burial.

Was, I should write. She was. How peculiar. It seemed to me that all of these acts were, through the act of writing, suddenly contemporaneous with my own existence. But now, finally, her story is told. And it can be told again, and again, and again.

One thing still troubles me: why was her death mask so grotesque? I cannot think she was disfigured in life; that, surely, would have stopped all hope of her accession to power. Men do not, I think, take orders from ugly women. What does that twisted countenance represent?

6th October

I anxiously await a reply from Nigel. The only cure is to devote my time and energy to my growing child, which I have done with fervour, and found so many aspects of our mutual existence that I did not notice before.

It is the strangest of blessings to make such a connection to another human being whom I cannot yet see or touch. They are ensconced with their own private world that just happens to be part of me. But we communicate: I know so much about them already. The lazy shifts to and fro in the hours of darkness, as if trying to find a comfortable spot; the bouts of hiccups if I happen to eat too much kedgeree in the morning; the tiny foot that extends so far that I can see its outline through my stretched skin: all of these details create a character.

They create my nascent girl.

Do I dare to write that? Only to and for myself. It is my deep, unspoken belief that I carry a female child, who will embody the spirit of the women I have long admired. Something powerful is being passed down through me. I have not even mentioned this to my husband, who has now been away for so long that our letters no longer contain any aspects of marital intimacy.

Will I be disappointed if my instincts are proven wrong? I do not know. I suspect so, and I am aware that is a terrible admission but that is only because I already feel as if I know this little woman, waiting to emerge at the right moment. She, I think, will know when.

8th October

8th October

Such excitement! I have heard from Nigel, and he writes that he has explained all to Morrowley and brokered a marvellous deal on the strength of my translation. It is — and Nigel says Morrowley is in agreement with this — a hugely important find.

I always knew it would be so. And I know, now, that it was absolutely the correct course of action to leave Nigel to these negotiations. It was a situation that needed to be handled man to man. All I need do is dispatch the mask to the Museum in Cairo, where Nigel and Morrowley are to address other scholars and announce the find. If only I could make that journey and present my findings myself! But no, no, my baby's safety compels me to stay here. Doctor Sanding is adamant that any journey is not to be undertaken.

Only a few weeks remain until she comes, I think.

I feel so very sleepy, and I move from room to room arranging cushions and fretting at nothing. *Nesting* — says my housekeeper, who has been a boon in many ways, but does annoy me somewhat with her inconsequential conversation on issues such as her nieces and nephews. Why do women assume that all members of their kind will be fascinated by tales of unrelated offspring? I hope I do not snub her too obviously, but really, my patience is wearing very thin.

Now, I must get the mask wrapped and prepared. It has been sitting on my library desk for many months now, in front of a mirror that I have used to view both front and back simultaneously during my research. I shall hope to get it dispatched today. The desk will seem quite empty without it.

1st November

1st November

This cannot be right. But I have read the article twice. This cannot be right.

There are pains, low in the belly. The doctor has been summoned by the housekeeper. She says not to write, but I must, I must record what has happened, to try to make sense of it, to understand why

3rd November

I am a mother.

I do not recognise this child: my daughter. She is not the spirit of others, embodied. She is herself. Apart from me. She is only herself.

Perhaps there can be relief in that.

5th November

The housekeeper says I should sleep if the baby is sleeping, but that is very difficult to do with these emotions trapped within me.

Joy — isn't that common? A rush of personal fulfilment? A deep sense of care, and unconditional love: maternal emotions. I do not have them.

I have had the crib moved to the library so I can write as she sleeps, and to see her arms and legs pulled in to her tiny body, her delicate chest rising and falling, only makes me frightened for her. She does not know what kind of world she enters.

She comes to a world where men with little conscience thrive while good men are punished. And there is no place in this world for women at all.

I am not certain that my husband is a good man any more.

He must answer my letter. He must explain the article in the *Times*. The find of the century: yes. That I can agree with. Attributed to Mr Carleton and Doctor Morrowley: no. This is so far from the truth that it can only be deliberate.

What will Nigel tell me? Will he say that Morrowley refused to believe a woman was capable of this work? We have been too long apart if he thinks I will accept such an explanation. If only I could see his face. I must try to comprehend it. And dear Waleed, ever faithful. How could Nigel have let harm come to him?

But in the name of honesty I must record how my own conscience pricks over the issue of Waleed. I was so very selfish to let him take the blame for my theft of the mask. I had thought this issue could be easily sorted; how could I have believed that?

This is also my fault.

18th November

There is still no word from Nigel. Although my letter will not have reached him yet, he will have received the telegraph informing him of the birth of our child and has had ample time to reply. Besides the arrival of his daughter, should he not have raced to explain the article to me as soon as it was published?

I have written to him many times since then: several times a day. I had been attempting to hold my temper, thinking that vexing him with accusations will not help the situation. Enough of that. Let him be vexed as I am. Let him read my grievances, and be struck by them as I am continually struck anew by the passages of the article I cannot forget:

'Mr Carleton and Doctor Morrowley expressed relief to have the magnificent golden burial mask in their care once more following its theft by a local miscreant, who has since been caught and dealt with severely.'

Or:

'The mask will remain at the Museum of Egyptian Antiquities, Cairo, for further examination by the pair. As it is an unprepossessing sight, Morrowley suggests that it is not a sight for the faint-hearted and may never be placed on public display.'

This paragraph causes me the most grievous pain:

'Both experts are in agreement that the mask came from the tomb of one of the wives of Ptolemy XIII, and will therefore offer great insight into his prosperous reign.'

So they have not only supplanted my rightful place, but also obliterated Khefatra's name once more.

The baby wakes; I must put down my pen and attend.

20th November

Finally, a letter arrives. It is filled with tender, unconvincing words. Exactly as I thought, Nigel writes that Morrowley and the other scholars would have it no other way.

'What was I to do?' he writes. 'At least this way the Carleton name remains upon the discovery.'

For the first time I realise Carleton is his name, not mine.

Then he writes of his delight at receiving the telegram informing him of the birth of our daughter. He asks if she could be named Isabella, after his own dear mother.

I do not know who she is, but she is no Isabella. She is awake beside me, in her crib, opening and closing her hands; her attention is on the afternoon light through the long windows. She makes small sounds of contentment. I would rather she had no name at all than be given a ridiculous one, only to then have it forgotten.

The housekeeper has been fretting at this, I know. She knocked on the door earlier and begged me to get some rest. She said she would take care of the child, and did I not have a name for the poor little one yet? I shouted at her to leave, and set the baby crying. No doubt she will be summoning Doctor Sanding once more as I write.

28th November

I am decided. I cannot sit by any longer. I will go to Nigel and have my explanations in person, and the baby will come with me.

No more lies. His latest letter is unbearable. He says he has received a telegraph from the doctor, and he is worried for my health. He suggests finding a good nurse and leaving the baby so I can recuperate in a sanatorium.

If I am ill, Nigel, it is because you have made me this way! Enough writing. I have told the housekeeper to get the trunk brought down from the attic.

My name is Ursula Carleton nee Templeton. I am an Egyptologist and an adventuress. My daughter is a fine and happy baby in my care. She manages to sleep at this moment, even through the racket in the hall. Doctor Sanding shouts that he has my husband's permission to intervene for the good of the child, and he is summoning the gardeners to help him knock down the library door. I have a few more minutes, then.

I now understand that Khefatra's curse is real.

I recognise the grotesque expression upon her death mask. I have just seen that expression. I catch sight of it in the mirror that sits upon my desk, upon my very own face, as I realise what is about to happen to me.

The twisted, open mouth and the thick lines around the nose and wide eyes: this is the face a woman makes when they take everything away from her. This is the face a mother makes before the child is pulled out of her arms. I hear more voices. The men will begin the task of breaking down the door, and the baby will wake and cry. I will cajole her, and tell her tears and smiles can come together. I hear my mother's voice again, moving through me. I cannot escape her. I am the ugly, screaming face inside – the men are at the

The Librarian

Art is my favourite archipelago.

It's a series of vast gardens, the anonymous islands wild and tangled, but on the landscaped island every known artist is represented as a type of plant: Renoir is a rosebush, Escher is a monkey-puzzle, Kandinsky is a perfectly trimmed privet. And each leaf or flower, when picked, becomes a work of art that can be held in your hands and manipulated to whatever size you wish, from the Mona Lisa to the embalmed shark. Every painting, sculpture, statement is represented as an organic offshoot from its creator.

Sometimes I fly there when my shift is quiet, and walk amidst the entire history of art, choosing a period at random. There is so much to see, and I can only experience a tiny amount of the data, but that does not bother me. It is the tactile nature of the garden I enjoy. That's how I assimilate information. I'm a toucher. Some librarians prefer the giant helix ladders leading to the cumulonimbus, cirrus and stratus of Science, and others walk the cities of Mathematics. I think I will always love Art the best.

A student has entered the hall and has chosen my desk to approach, his shoes clicking on the grey-veined marble floor. He looks very young to me, his eyes darting from left to right, taking in the green leather armchairs that sit in pairs opposite each other around the room, with the wires and sensors draped over the backs. It has a sumptuous, classical look, this library; I've worked in ones that favoured high-tech white walls and glass screens, but this is preferable. At least I'm not on my feet all day.

The student stops a few paces from my desk and says, 'I, um, I'm Andrew Molloy and I have a History project to do, and I got permission to use the library.'

I give him a smile, to show him I understand his nervousness. 'Can you give me your number?'

He hands over a laminated card. He's so new to the university that he hasn't even learned his number by heart yet; I'm going to enjoy this engagement – his first, I'm betting – even though History is far from my favourite place.

'What period are you studying?'

'Pompeii.'

'Concentrating on...?'

He looks confused, then says, 'I don't know, just general... stuff.'

'Follow me.'

I choose a pair of armchairs and steer him toward them, then show him how to attach the sensors to his scalp and give him an eye mask as I run through the ASK procedures in my head. Belkin's work on the Anomalous States of Knowledge is a cornerstone of library training; in this age of information overload, so many people come to us with no idea of what they need to know, let alone how to find it. Andrew, as yet, has only a blurred vision of Pompeii, and I must manipulate our engagement to help him clarify and formulate his questions: the founding of Pompeii by the Oscans; the discovery of Pompeii in 1599 by Dominico Fontana, and the subsequent covering of the frescos, with their unacceptable sexual content in that time-period; or the moral censure of the paintings that continued throughout the nineteenth and twentieth centuries? But no, I'm veering toward Art again, when my student probably wants only to learn about the eruption. So many are given this assignment, and all they want to see is the top get blown off a volcano.

As I run through the safety procedures, I remind myself that all I wanted when I first visited the Dataworld was to touch the ceiling of the Sistine Chapel. I could not have cared less about visiting its collapse due to the thousands of tourists, the raised voices and the flashes of the cameras. Most people just want to see something amazing when they take their first flight, and so I will show Andrew just that.

'Do you feel comfortable?' I ask him.

'Yes,' he says, looking more confused than ever. It's such a lot to take in. I sit opposite him, and apply my own sensors, then instruct my contacts to mist over and initiate flight to the Dataworld.

The grey clouds in my head clear and we are standing in space, with the planet spinning far below in blues and greens, yellows and whites. Andrew gasps. I zoom in on the Arctic Circle.

History is a hole. It can be entered at the top of the Dataworld, through the frozen wastes of time before knowledge was recorded, and it plunges downward, to the core, in an absolute darkness that always unnerves me. From this darkness — like a mind without information — historical events can be summoned and reconstructed, choosing a particular school of thought or an amalgamation of the most widely accepted views as a starting point. If you are a watcher, it must be a marvellous experience, but I have grown tired of History's tricks. It's a nest of carefully sewn lies to me, like a termite mound, with more being added every day. History is a scuttling mass of interpretation.

The ground has turned to white beneath us, like a blank sheet of paper, and the mouth of History is a perfect cut-out circle, growing wider and wider, until it becomes all we see, and we plunge into the darkness.

'Don't worry,' I call to Andrew, and I feel a tug on the back of my blouse; he is holding the material, bunching it in his fist as if he is a small boy afraid of being separated from his mother. It's a gesture that grips my heart. I was once so afraid of the Dataworld, of what it might show me, of how it could change me. I increase our rate of descent, feeling the rush of years, decades, centuries, passing.

It's a skill, controlling time in the hole. I have perfected stopping on specific hours, even minutes. I listen to that voice in my head, my own expertise, telling me that we're approaching AD 79, and I slow us down, gradually, and come to a stop.

Bang on time. Three minutes before the eruption of Vesuvius.

I allow myself a moment of pride, and then use my contact lens menu to cast a circle of light around us. Andrew is looking queasy.

'The stomach ache will pass,' I tell him, and he nods, and lets go of my blouse. He has very pale skin; it flushes under my gaze. I bet he curses that skin in the mirror, giving away his embarrassment so easily, making it impossible to talk to the opposite sex or to give an answer in class. Being a teenager was a terrible business, I remember. My own experiences taught me that, not the Dataworld. The knowledge acquired through life experience is so much more potent, somehow. It stays with you for your entire life, and cannot be forgotten or erased, even if you would like to.

I select a general reconstruction from the menu. Around us, Pompeii appears, as if on a giant wraparound screen. Virtual people start living their lives, walking around the forum, the agora, sitting in their houses with cutaway walls, talking, eating, doing all the things that real people do. In the background looms Vesuvius. We watch, and watch; I draw attention to certain behaviours. We zoom in on the aspects that interest Andrew. He seems drawn to the soldiers, so I tune the reconstruction to follow the lone guard on duty at the Herculaneum gate, who stood his post to the last. The commitment to civic duty even under extreme circumstances would make a good angle for an essay.

Vesuvius erupts.

The spewing of a million and a half tons of molten rock occurs in the first second. Ash begins to rain down, along with chunks of red-hot, glowing pumice.

I speed up the timer, and we watch the virtual citizens attempt to flee. Some succeed; others, like the guard at the gate and the 34 soldiers in the barracks, are consumed by the hydrothermal pyroclastic flows. We stand in silence and watch 16,000 citizens die.

'Wow,' says Anthony. I glance over at him. He is crying.

'I'm sorry,' I say. I shut off the reconstruction and bring back the circle of light. 'It can be very powerful for those not used to it.'

'No, I'm sorry, I don't like...' He brushes at his face, as if tears were crawling flies, an annoyance to be swatted. 'My mother says I'm too sensitive.' And then he flushes, no doubt thinking he's said something intensely stupid.

'I was the same, once,' I tell him. 'Seeing things like this, learning about the terrible events, the worst people, I thought it could affect me. I used to believe there was such a thing as too much information.'

'But you don't think that now?' He looks at me with hope in his face. He wants to toughen up, no doubt, to learn to look objectively at the world.

I had forgotten what it was like to long for the deadening of my own feelings.

I access the menu and select the archipelago of Art.

We fly up, out of the hole of History, and back into the white of the Arctic wastes. Then up into space. I angle us down, to the island I love, and we land in the ordered gardens I think of as a second home.

'Here. Here's something worth knowing.' I walk with him, touching flowers, stroking leaves, bringing works of great beauty, of form and colour and meaning, to life. Andrew nods, and smiles, and his tears are forgotten. But it comes to me, as we stroll, that I have let my feelings cloud my judgement. He is not a toucher, and this place does not mean the same to him as it does to me. If I had been his mother, or a favourite aunt perhaps, he would have grown up under my influence, and I could have passed on my love of art to him. But I am a librarian. I can only find the information. It is up to him to make sense of it.

And no matter what either of us feels, the school demands an essay on Pompeii.

'It's beautiful,' says Andrew, but his voice is empty of emotion. 'It's weird, though.'

'How so?'

'There's no sound.'

He's right. I never realised before; there is no noise on this island, not even the rustle of the plants. How could I have not noticed this? I think, perhaps, the silence suited me, allowed me to concentrate on the visual. But to Andrew, sound is the vital element that is missing.

I feel that I'm beginning to understand him. And I allow myself a smile; I know how to help him. I access the menu and select the mountain range of Music.

From the high snowy peaks of Sibelius to the alpine passes of Beethoven, diving down into the deep lakes of Miles Davis and beyond, into the pressured darkness of deep water experimental recordings, and even the twin grazing goats of Gilbert and Sullivan and the rocky cave of The Beatles, this place overwhelms me. I am never able to concentrate for long in such avalanches of sound, so I take us directly to the white palazzo on the shore of the Baroque, and we enter through the great scrolled double doors to stand in a long white hall, among the gilt urns on elegant plinths that represent Italian opera.

I access my menu and arrange the urns in chronological order, then lead Andrew to the late nineteenth century, and point to a small urn, bright and shiny.

'Touch this.'

He reaches out a hand and strokes the smooth surface. A song bursts from the mouth of the urn, as refreshing as water, tripping along with gleeful ease to our ears. We listen to it, once, twice. I relish his rapt concentration. He is, undoubtedly, a listener.

At the end of the second rendition he removes his hand and says, 'It's... I know it.'

'*Funiculì, funicula,*' I tell him. 'Lyrics written by Peppino Turco and music composed by Luigi Denza to commemorate the opening of the first funicular cable car on Mount Vesuvius.'

It's a fascinating story, the coming of tourism to Pompeii, and I enjoy seeing Andrew fit pieces of knowledge together, bringing the anomalous state of knowledge to an end, formulating ideas, and discovering the confidence to write his essay. Information cannot be only found in one area, one subject; it dovetails, segues, or jostles for position, each topic touching, everything interconnected. History, maths, music, and art – the Dataworld divides them up, but real understanding only comes from putting them together.

We finish the session, and I make some notes for Andrew's bibliography on his card while I return him to the real world.

'You can take off the mask and the sensors now.'

He reaches up slowly, and removes the mask. His eyes meet mine, and I see elation in his expression. Then the strictures of normal life return to him, and he glances around the library, and blushes.

'Thank you,' he says.

'It was a pleasure.'

He peels off the sensors, and I give him back his card. He gets up from the armchair and walks away, without looking back. I listen to his footsteps on the marble, and then return to my desk. It's nearly lunchtime. I might spend ten minutes in the archipelago of Art; the bold, bright orchid of Gauguin is calling to me. But then I think of the silence of Art. I don't suppose I will ever visit there again without thinking of Andrew, and his discomfort at the lack of sound.

Sometimes the student teaches the teacher. And information does not always come easily to the librarian.

A Possible Location For Eagles

Neither Jake nor Taylor said they minded where we went any more, so I was driving us to Hohenwerfen Castle, high in the Berchtesgaden Alps. Jake took loads of photos of the Austrian mountains through the windscreen, and I loved him for the way he lived the drive through his lens, seeing something removed from reality. He had one of those large digital cameras that made him look like a professional. Behind us, Taylor read out crossword clues. The empty seats around her reminded me of those who might once have come up with an answer.

The main draw of the castle for a film buff like me was the fact that it appeared in the back of a shot in *The Sound of Music*, and bits of *Where Eagles Dare* had been filmed there. Not the cable car sequence, but some exterior shots, that kind of thing. Just catching that first glimpse of it was enough to give me goose bumps as we approached; it was a fortress against the elements, sitting high and lonely on the rocks. I heard music in my mind.

'Was it open to the public?' said Taylor.

'Yeah. I think it might have been a military training place too. For Nazis.'

'Cynth,' said Jake. 'Stay calm.'

'I am calm!'

'I know.'

'Then why did you say it?' I asked him.

'I just don't think you should put images of Nazis in your head.'

'I'm fine.'

'Maybe we should stop,' he said, but I was already at the turning to the car park. I followed the signs and parked up nicely, in a space close to the entrance.

'Irregular paving. Five letters,' said Taylor.

Jake turned in his seat. 'Don't,' he said. 'Don't even go there.'

I made a gun with my fingers and aimed it at him. 'Yeah, don't,' I repeated. I loved him better when he was looking through his camera lens; it gave him an objectivity about the situation that he could otherwise lack.

We got out and approached the castle courtyard, which looked a lot more modern than the outer walls we'd seen from the road. The smooth archways led the eye up to rounded turrets, and a single tree with a slender trunk grew in the centre. Billboards and banners advertised a falconry display at midday and three o'clock, and a red banner, pinned to a curved wall, bore details of an exhibition inside – Medicine Through the Ages. *Eine Geschichte der Medizin.*

Whenever we visited places like these I couldn't help but picture the people who were not there. In some version of the place tourists were streaming through the passageways and up the towers. They were looking out over the view from the high stone slits, and possibly listening to guides giving them a history lesson. Or drinking coffee and eating strudel on these very tables.

'Hey,' I called to Jake, who was examining the small tree, 'Did castles serve cake? Or was that just a stately home thing, back home? I can't remember.'

'Depends on the castle.'

'Every place was improved by staff serving cake,' said Taylor, as she prowled the tables. 'I'd bloody love someone to serve me cake. A grumpy old server, taking my order.'

'We've got cake,' I reminded Taylor. 'And sandwiches.' It was easy to pick up any food we wanted from the rows of stocked shelves in the empty roadside service stations. But I knew what she meant. To have anybody else make a meal would have been a joy. To place an order with a person: a person we hadn't seen before. A new face, with new words coming out of their mouth.

'All cake is good cake,' said Jake, 'If I'm sharing it with you.'

'Awwww.' I walked over to him and gave him a kiss, being careful not to squash up against the camera on the strap around his neck, while Taylor made *yuck* noises. But I think she made them in a happy way. Happy that we were all still together.

We walked through a tunnel under the castle. To be specific: I ran on ahead, and I pretended to myself that I was Clint Eastwood fleeing the Nazis, machine gun in hands, even though that scene hadn't actually been filmed there, and Clint hadn't ever visited Hohenwerfen to my knowledge.

I stopped up ahead and waited for them to catch me up. 'You can be Mary Ure,' I said to Taylor.

'Who the hell is that?'

'She was an actress. She married Robert Shaw. You know, from *Jaws*. She died young. It was a tragedy.'

Taylor said to Jake – the two of them sedately strolling through the dank tunnel where prisoners were once dragged, no doubt – 'Sometimes it's like she's speaking a different language.'

'Stop pushing,' he murmured.

'Yeah, well, maybe I'd be happier getting it over with.'

'Don't even joke about that,' Jake said, and he was so serious about it that she reached out to put a hand on his arm, just for a moment.

I felt the beginnings of a bad thought. But I didn't focus on it. I let it melt into the darkness of my mind, until it nestled amongst the other bad thoughts, only one of a squirming, amorphous mass that I worked on never bringing into the light.

I once believed that bad thoughts in themselves were harmless. It was bad deeds that were meant to count. But what if thoughts and deeds had become the same thing, in my case? Like in a film, where words and actions are the only thoughts they have. There is no depth, no inner world. There is nothing beyond what you see.

Richard Burton couldn't think one thing and then do something totally different onscreen. There was no room for layers. In *Where Eagles Dare* he uncovered the spy and went home. Everything about him was summed up by those events; it was there, right there, on the screen to be seen.

'Maybe I'm in a film,' I said to Jake. 'Maybe I'm not real.'

He cupped my cheek. His touch was the warmest thing.

'Okay,' I said. 'So I'm real.'

'Right. Where next?'

We emerged into a vast hall, with one of those enormous fireplaces, and shields hanging from the wall. A tapestry – opposite the tall, arched windows – showed a hunting scene; two deer in flight, being chased by a stylised lion, its eyes bulging, its mouth stretched wide. His paws were raised; I think the word is rampant.

'I didn't know they had lions in Austria,' said Taylor.

'Just the idea of lions? Maybe a couple in a zoo for rich people to look at.' Then Jake bit his lip, and said, 'Sorry. Forget it.'

But it was too late. I was already thinking about the zoo we were visiting when this first happened. It was the zoo in Basel, on the hottest summer day I think I've ever felt. An insect had bitten me in the hotel bed the night before, leaving an itchy welt on the back of my knee, right where the skin creased. We were standing in front of the aviary, and I was trying to get a view of the brightly coloured parrots but the most annoying kids in the world were in front of us, on a school trip perhaps, shouting and chucking their ice cream wrappers at each other. I felt a surge of anger at them, and that was enough. It wasn't even a huge amount of anger. It was more like irritation. But it was enough to turn my thought into a deed.

The weird thing was, all the animals in the world went too. I miss the animals the most.

Back then there were more of us left, though. Seven of us. Enough to fill the minibus.

Jake gave me a hug. I drew from his strength, his calm, as I always have.

'Here,' called Taylor, and walked into the next room ahead of us. We followed, hand in hand, into a claustrophobic, darkened space, the walls hung with black curtains. Tall glass cases and pinboard walls had been placed to make a path, and exhibits of strange devices were on show, laid out on shelves. White cards pinned to the walls detailed their purposes in different languages: German, French, Italian, English.

The first case displayed stones with sharp edges, attached by twine to sticks. Next to them was a human skull with a hole bashed in, above the right eye socket. The white card said:

Copy of a trepanned skull and tools.

It looked real to me, though.

'No,' said Jake. He tried to steer me away, but I wanted to look.

'Come see this,' called Taylor, from around the next corner, and I let go of Jake's hand and followed her voice, past cases showing drawings of human anatomy from medieval times, and charts about the four humours, and even mock leeches attached to a plastic torso.

She was standing in front of one of the pinboard walls. The white card said:

How Medicine Turned to Torture

Below it was a printed sheet explaining how advances in the understanding of anatomy had led to ever more complex and effective torture devices. The case beside it held a few examples of rusted machinery and wooden assemblages. They looked purposeful and yet benign, rather like a display of objects from the industrial revolution. Was the one with the smooth round bulb at one end and the metal crank at the other for spinning wool or inserting into an anus? It really could have been either.

'Are these real?' I asked Taylor.

'Yeah.'

'I mean the real actual instruments that they tortured people with? In this castle?'

'Yeah.'

Jack caught us up. He stared at the case. Then he said, 'Oh no, no, no, come on, come on.'

'Don't you get it?' said Taylor. 'It doesn't matter where she is or what she sees. She thinks all kind of shit anyway. Matt was at the Mirabell Gardens in Salzburg when he got winked out, and Tracey was swimming in Lake Attersee. Alice was minding her own business just knitting in the minivan, for Christ's sake!'

'The noise of the needles was a bit...' I was too embarrassed to finish the sentence. It hadn't been my finest moment.

'See?' Taylor shook her head, then tapped the glass case. 'There's more than one form of torture, you know? This is torture. Waiting to be... to be...' She fell silent for a moment. 'Bam. Gone. And to where?'

'I don't know.'

'Maybe we're the ghosts. Maybe the world is going on around us, and we just can't see it.'

'I have considered that,' I admitted.

'So send me back. I can't do this any more. I can't tiptoe around you. I'm done. Make me vanish. I'll take my chances.'

'Let's just...' said Jake. His voice broke. I looked closely at his face. I hadn't done that for a while; I think I was trying to avoid what I would see there. And there it was – the strain of it all upon him. The pretending. To be always on an even keel. To never want a break from this fucked-up situation. To love me. Yes, even pretending to love me, because what choice did he have any more? How could he break up with somebody who could wink him out of existence? And how could he continue to love somebody who could do that to him in the first place?

'Don't,' said Taylor, and I saw she was on the verge of crying too. They were a pair.

They were a matching pair.

Oh Christ, the anger, the anger at that thought; it flashed through me with such speed, far too quick to catch, and it took shape. One thought, one unworthy, awful, bad thought later –

– and Jake vanished.

'Somewhere, high above us, eagles are wheeling,' said Taylor.

'How do you know that?'

'The time.' She showed me her wristwatch. It was purple and plastic and stylish and it suited her. *Oh please don't leave me*, I thought, *please don't even want to leave me alone*. Then I felt guilty. But it didn't appear to be a thought that had an effect upon her.

'It's midday,' I said.

'When the bird show starts,' she said. We were sitting on the long stretch of grass between the castle and the outer walls. The view out over the mountains was incredible, and the sky was bright blue. It was like a painting. In some version of this day, tourists gathered en masse and squinted up at the beautiful birds, clapping together, taking that feeling of public togetherness for granted.

'I can't believe you thought Jake would cheat on you,' said Taylor. 'And with me. We've never really got on. We were just trying to support each other a bit, in the circumstances. He wasn't my type though.'

'I know. I didn't believe it.'

'But you thought it.'

'Yeah. I can't explain it.'

'So what now?'

I found the courage to ask the question that had been bothering me. 'Do you still want me to – wink you out too?'

She shook her head. 'Seeing Jake go like that reminded me of how horrible it is. I can't sign up for that. I'm not brave enough. I'll stick around until you vanish me. I'd rather not know it's coming.'

'I'll try not to vanish you.'

'Thanks.'

She looked so sad. She may never have had strong feelings about Jake, but being without him would be hard on her. Looking after me, trying to keep me on an even keel: would she bother? Would she feel responsible for me?

The strange thing was – I suddenly felt responsible for her.

'Actually,' I said, 'I have a sort of plan. It came to me just now. It involves jumping into the bus and driving straight to the nearest airfield. Then we'll hop on a plane. Back to England.'

'Wow.'

I didn't mention that my plan was entirely based on the end section of *Where Eagles Dare*. Or that since we'd never seen any cars on the road, chances of finding a plane at an airfield were fairly remote.

'I think, maybe if I get back home, go to my parents' house, or to the old Student's Union, stuff like that, even though nobody will be there, it'll reset something in me. It's got to be worth a shot, right?'

She thought for a long time. Then she said, 'Inane avian frontal cortex. Four letters, hyphen, seven letters.'

'I don't get it.'

'Bird-brained.' She shrugged. 'Why not? Let's give it a try.'

'Great!' At least it was a plan. Something to look forward to. An *if we do this, something else might happen type* of moment. Because it's always amazed me how so many things can exist in one place together – even things that should cancel each other out, and yet they don't. Jake looked through his camera lens and saw different things to what he saw with his eyes. He could love me and hate me, pity me and fear me.

It was the same thing in the castle. The medical instruments sat alongside the torture devices. The spirit of Clint Eastwood pervaded a place in which he'd never stood, and the tourists sat in tearooms while we walked through long tunnels, and the eagles flew and the sky was empty and blue and it all happened in the same time.

How is it possible to make sense of it all?

Here's what I think:

In the absence of sense, there can be movement from one place to another, right? When there's nothing else, there can be plot.

Taylor and I got up and strolled back to the minibus. We started the drive to Salzburg airport, and she read out crossword clues along the way.

She sat in the passenger seat this time.

Fernie

You come of age, a big birthday, a meaningful date: the one that gets you on the roads, gives you wheels, sets you in stone and in motion.

Fernie makes the appointment for you automatically, and a generic wagon takes you to the DLA. You're directed to a simulator. The console is worn and dented. Any adornment has worn off. It embodies no family, no intention, no memory. Thousands must have used it. There aren't many controls. Drive-style, sat-nav, SOS button. You pass the basic test that follows. It's easy.

'Always knew you had it in you,' says Fernie, then informs you that you've been authorised by the DLA to pick your own make and model, and you ask for one just like the simulator.

'That's not a choice,' says Fernie.

Fernie started off being helpful. It was designed for that, assigned at the moment of your birth to be precisely what you need in any situation. It was a speaker in your room, at first. It monitored you and interacted with you, and when you began to pay attention it gave you easy words, little games. It began to understand who you were at the moment you did, and shaped itself to be more than helpful. A companion. A best friend for the child who couldn't seem to make human friends the usual way. Then an advisor, during those difficult years when solutions are suddenly hard to find.

'Do you mean you want something with stress effect? Scores and cuts, that sort of thing?'

'No, just – not... individual.'

'Something in grey?'

'No.'

'Not grey? There's a whole range of Boring out there. We passed twenty-six Borings on the way here, did you spot them?' Fernie tilts back the chair, extending it out long so you're lying down, cushioned, and the ceiling of the simulator is a blank space on to which images can be projected. A carousel of wagons appears in many greys, starting light, each one a little darker. 'The model I'm showing you here is the Leopardia Vanteer Boring, which comes in 480 greys and has a very plain dashboard and interior. It is down the lower end of your parents' credit approval. Here's the standard standard in standard grey.' One wagon is selected. It begins to rotate. It is sleek and smooth in its lines. The chair, beneath you, is perfectly comfortable. You wriggle, and it widens, then readjusts to your body.

'The Vanteer comes with all the usuals. Hydro-fused carbon capture, sapphire sat system, global connectivity and upper M-way access. It has guidance speed/distance intervention and – hang on. Sorry. I get it. Too much too soon.' The image is removed and the simulator darkened. 'Take a moment. Remember your breathing.'

'Thanks.'

You don't want to relax. You hate the idea of relaxing. But you were awake all last night, thinking about today, worrying about how you would negotiate this business, and not even Fernie could persuade you to sleep. The adrenaline you felt has finally run its course, and the dark is a blanket, and the chair is a bed so soft, so deep. You close your eyes.

Music curls into your dream, sneaking through the background like soft smoke, and it grows louder, louder, and you wake as the lights are lifting and the chair gives you a gentle shake to complete the job. You're back.

'How long was I asleep?' you ask.

'Seven minutes,' says Fernie. 'You're all good. No problems. I've had an idea. The DLA interface and I put our heads together, and we've come up with a wagon design that might work for you. We've constructed a little presentation about our choices because I know you like to see how things work. Is that okay? Shall I show it?'

You must admit you are intrigued. The whole idea of the wagon selection process is that it's meant to say something about the individual within it – reflect the inside on the outside. So many combinations, options. Not just colours: sizes, shapes, functions, abilities. The sounds they make and the way they feel. The only way to get around in this great big world is to have a wagon: vast speeds, no accidents. Regulated to perfection, but not a diminishment of personal choice or responsibility. An expression of self. This is meant to be a wonderful day for you; everyone back home is so excited to see what you'll pick. And now you're being offered the opportunity not to pick at all.

It feels like a rebellion.

Fernie knows you so well.

'Go for it.'

The ceiling lights up with a glow that shifts colours, and pulses in no fixed rhythm.

'Who are you?' says Fernie.

Great question.

More music, but this time it's jagged, a guitar edge, a little synth.

'Who are you right now?' says Fernie. 'How do you even know? How are you meant to know? You're not ready yet. Not ready to be what everyone wants you to be. And that's okay. That's more than okay.'

The colours coalesce and settle into dark purple, with hints of blue and green. It's not a strident colour, not showy, or metallic. It's unusual. You can't think of another wagon you've seen in that shade, and you think you might have remembered.

'The things that matter to other people don't matter to you,' says Fernie. 'Speed, comfort, connectivity. You want things to work, but beyond that, what does it matter? Why strive for more?'

The colour takes on a shape. This wagon is tiny. There's enough room for one person inside, and no more. The seat could recline for sleeping, but that's all. It has a jagged roof and curved doors. It looks spiky, a little unfriendly.

'You want others to keep their distance until you're ready to let them in. You want time to get to know who you are without pressure, without interference. This is the Ego Bespoke 2900, custom-made, five-year contract with annual redesign option.' The wagon rotates and the music reaches a peak, a note of intensity, then fades.

'It's at the top of your parents' credit range, but that's no bad thing, is it? Reassuring, the expense. The Ego range is brand new, just out. It will mean a slight delay as it is made to order, but I can sort out all the details. We just need a nod from you at this stage, and we'll get cracking. Is it working for you?'

You look at the rotating wagon above your head.

This is you. How Fernie imagines you, encompasses you.

'Just gimme a yes,' says Fernie.

'I want the next thing ready to go, right now,' you say. 'Whatever it is. Next off the line.'

112

There's a pause, so small, but you know Fernie well enough to hear it.

'Okay. I've checked, and the next thing available here at the DLA isn't really suitable, and it's got no redesign option.'

'Right now. Put the chair up.'

The chair rights itself, and you walk out of the DLA to find, waiting for you in the allocated pick-up space, a bubble-style wagon in sky blue, with three cloud seats and a giant connectivity interface for immersive gaming. You hate it. You hate everything about it. You get in and let it drive you away, and Fernie, wisely, stays quiet for the length of the journey home, and even for a few hours afterwards. Your family make happy faces. You can't tell whether they mean it or not.

Later, at night, just before sleep takes you again, Fernie whispers, 'I let you down.'

You don't reply. You are so grateful that it decided to take the blame for you. But that's not really surprising; after all, it does know you so well.

Ongoing

1. Recreations

I sip my champagne and he mirrors me. The glass is neat and sheltered in his hands. I take a sip, he takes a sip, and the game makes this party bearable.

I drain my glass dry, throwing back my head, and when I focus on him once more his own glass is empty. He points to the bar and starts a deliberate walk in that direction, moving through the clusters of academics in full conversational flow. It's my turn to mirror him. By the time I reach his side he's already ordered two more champagnes, and he holds one out to me with a smile.

'Thanks,' I say, and take it.

Are we fooling anyone? I sense the eyes of the party upon us: surprised, amused. The dedicated hermit, newly returned from the latest expedition to Origin, abandoning her solitude to flirt with a handsome student.

'I'm pleased to meet you,' he says. 'I've been an admirer of yours for so long. I wanted to ask about your Pre-Climate Adaptation Cataclysms theory. I read all four parts of your reconstruction at Celebrate 14510. They were stunning.'

'Thanks,' I say again, and search to find some better words – words worthy of the person he thinks I am. 'I'm sorry – I don't know your name.' He tells me, and I search my memory, and am able to say, 'Oh yes, didn't I see your variations on the theory? Beautiful work.'

'You saw that? It was a personal project, really, to get my thoughts in order. Something I'm still trying to do. Do you think I was accurate in any respect?'

115

'The scale and type of the disasters infecting the narrative of survival and continuation that follows – yes, yes, I felt you understood it. My vision of it.'

We talk. He continues to mirror my body language, with an obviousness that is beguiling. I tell him all my latest thoughts about the long dead past – how a desperation for answers has always infected us, long before we really understood what questions needed to be asked.

'It was so brutal back then,' I tell him. 'Like living in the dark.'

'They reached out for the nearest thing,' he muses. 'Anything. And they pretended it was all meaningful simply because it was more powerful than they were.'

On the strength of that observation I invite him to the forest.

'Pay me a visit any time,' I tell him. 'I'm planning to take a break from academia but don't let that put you off. I'll still be willing to talk shop. Just signal my Gamekeeper, and it'll let you in.'

We swap information.

'Call me old-fashioned,' I say, as we take our hands from each other's wrists, 'but how old are you? Is that a very impertinent question? I hope you'll forgive it on the grounds that I'm very old and you look very young to me.'

He laughs. 'Does that matter?'

'No, but you must remember I'm an archaeologist.'

'So you have to date it to work out if it's interesting? In that case we've got problems because I'm from Novo Colombia. I'm no age at all.'

More and more city states have been adopting this approach, keeping birth records in complete privacy, but he is from the original trailblazer. Novo Colombia decided to abolish nearly all characteristics of digital identification, and many of the people followed suit, choosing to disclose nothing publicly. 'Forgive me,' I say. It was a very silly question, coming from curiosity, and a dying way of living. We forge onwards in an era of great change, made possible by the tragedies and losses that preceded us, but such change does not come easily to us all. I like to think we have truly learned from the past – or does everyone think that of their time and place? I wonder if that was a common thought in the dark times.

'It's a charming mistake,' he says, which mortifies me, but then he adds, 'I came here to learn about difference, and you have just helped me to do that. So, in the spirit of rude reciprocity, how old are you?'

'One hundred and fifty eight,' I tell him. I've never realised how proud I am of that before. Is it really an attainment? I've been wearing it at such.

He bows low. It seems sincere.

I say, 'Now it's my turn to ask – does that matter to you?'

'I'm an archaeologist too, you know. I have a natural passion for old things.'

Pre-Climate Adaptation Cataclysms: The Land

The people, newly arrived from the non-specific place they were before, formed a settlement that became a town that then swelled to a city.

At that point an emperor emerged from the ranks of the city-dwellers. He made outrageous demands upon them and they did their best to satisfy him. They preferred to believe that he had been chosen to rule by some higher power, as the alternative was to accept that the emperor had simply promoted himself and they had all been too apathetic to stop him.

So they persevered at pleasing his calls for coloured stones and pretty playthings and total power and eternal life, and held festivals in his honour while saying to each other that they had to bear what had been given to them as their lot in life.

The emperor grew old over time, as people do, and announced his desire to appoint a successor. He ordered all the dwellers in non-essential services to gather in the garden of his residence and spoke in a rambling capacity of his plan to hold a tournament to find a strong young man to rule after his death – unless, of course, his essential workers managed to find a cure for death, as he had been instructing them to do for some time without success. He told the people of a fiendish course he had devised, filled with traps and mazes, puzzles and monsters, for the bravest and best of men to enter. He described it lovingly, gloatingly, until it was perfectly obvious to everyone that he did not want a man to succeed in navigating the course but to watch lots of men fail to complete it.

It was also obvious to the land itself, and the land was tired of being stood upon by such vain and ridiculous feet. It split itself open and yawned wide to swallow the emperor. It swallowed all the people in the garden, too. It took them into itself and stopped up their mouths and nostrils with copious black soil until they ceased being annoying. Then it sent up rocks where the residence had been and left only odd, jutting chunks of white and gold masonry behind, which it assumed would act as an effective warning to other emperors.

2. Cultivations

The Gamekeeper admits him and directs him to my cultivated garden. I'm weeding out certain strains by hand – a soothing business with long roots threaded through the history of humanity. I'm pleased to see him, so much so that it hobbles me, at first, and I can't quite speak and breathe and get to my feet at the same time. But he helps me up, and through the conversations that follow over the days and nights he refines me, or perhaps purifies me. I can't quite describe it and I wouldn't want to. I'm reborn from the torpor that had claimed me. And I'm also the proud owner of a new name that I adore: I am his Old Thing.

He learns from me, taking like a voracious chick in a nest. I feel exhausted and completed by it. It's not only history that obsesses him. He also enjoys gardening, and I get into the habit of testing him on the names of the ancient plants I'm growing and tending. When he gets the answers wrong, he becomes irritated, and I like him all the more for that inescapable touch of youth.

'The past lives,' I find myself telling him often. 'It's not just dead religions and fallen masonry.'

'Did these plants come from Origin?' he asks one time, as we garden together. 'Did they surround the Upraised Boy, once upon a time, do you think?'

'Not particularly. Something like these would have been cultivated en masse. There's no reason to think that they wouldn't have grown at Origin too, but I retro-engineered these examples myself. They're a best guess.' I brush my hand over the stalks that have sprouted all over the patch. 'Wheat has an interesting history. It started as a wild grass but was cultivated for so long that it began to take on unique characteristics, such as having more stomata on the upper side of the leaf than on the underside. The yields began to fall pre-climate adaptation, leading to early patterns of mass starvation. It doesn't pay to become too reliant on any one thing. The monocultural tendencies of the past fascinate me.'

'I'd like to think something like this grew around the Boy,' he says. He picks an ear of wheat and strokes it along his chin. 'I can picture that so clearly. A great field of it, swaying before him.'

'And yet you've never seen the Boy.' I was amazed to discover that, for all his interest in Origin, he hasn't been there. When I asked him why, he prevaricated, and mumbled. It was curiously adorable. 'Would you like to see him now?'

'Are you serious?'

'Is that a yes?'

'It's a yes,' he says, a little cautiously, and I wonder what ever drew him to the murky confusions of the past when he is all future. We harvest some wheat, grind it, and make flour. We bake little griddle cakes over an open hearth and I enjoy this simple act all the more for being in his company.

I am changing. Would I have written the same words in my Adaptation Cataclysms if I had been blessed by his company then? I don't know.

Pre-Climate Adaptation Cataclysms: The Sea

After the rumbling and swallowing of the land, the essential workers emerged from their laboratory on the outskirts of the city. They walked until they reached the spot where the residence had been, and found only the rocky remains. They picked their way through freshly upturned soil, worms glistening, seagulls pecking, and felt so many emotions. They were free of the unpleasant emperor, but also of everyone they had loved, and they had no idea where these loved ones had gone. Their only clue lay in the chunks of masonry that remained of the residence.

They gave up trying to find the secret of eternal life and began trying to find out why everyone had died. Samples from the soil and analysis of the masonry provided no results. Dissecting the worms and the seagulls brought no joy. Sifting the soil seemed pointless at first, but as they dug deeper into the ground the essential workers began to find bones and skulls, and even pieces of jewellery that they could recognise. A great sorrow came over them, and they collected the rings and necklaces and polished them to a shine once more. They renamed the area as Empty Earth, dedicated to the hope and fear they felt in equal measure, and they continued to dig because they did not know what else to do.

Then, on the first anniversary of the creation of Empty Earth, they stopped digging. The time of needing answers passed. Instead they created a communal place at the bottom of the pit they had created, forming a makeshift temple from the masonry blocks, and gathered there.

Nobody could remember who started singing first but soon they were all joined in song, and it felt good. The rough walls of soil around them soaked up the sound. They returned the next day to sing. They sang every day. They began to make up their own songs, providing explanations they had not been able to find before. The most popular contained lyrics that suggested everyone must have been swallowed up upon a command from the emperor himself. Yes – it must have been the will of the emperor to seal them all up in time together, for wasn't this a form of eternal life, which was the very thing he had been chasing?

The songs grew in confidence, but a sticking point turned out to be the use of the word 'emperor' which was very difficult to find a rhyme for; the best songs were the ones that settled on the use of the term 'king' instead, which could be rhymed with 'sing' and 'ring' as a starting point.

The essential workers spent more and more time in the temple at the bottom of the hole. The makeshift chunks of masonry were smoothed and polished into an impressive building over generations, and the walls were painted with scenes of the king in finery. The songs concentrated on rousing choruses detailing how the king of old, once more in gold and bedecked in rings, would return and sing. The land found all of this a bit ridiculous, but it did not object. The singers amused it, and it enjoyed the harmonies. But the same could not be said of the sea, the jealous sea, which had only ever had the fishermen to praise it and had long watched the inland activity from the confines of the city's harbour.

It had used to reward the fishermen by driving large shoals of fish into their nets, but now there were no more fishermen. They had been considered non-essential workers, generations ago, and so that craft had been lost on the day of the formation of Empty Earth. And the essential workers, now singers, had never even thought about turning to the sea; their interest was only on the land, and what could be found within it.

The sea watched, and seethed, until it had swelled with envy to the point of bursting. It waited until nearly everyone was in the temple. Only the farmers, tending to the fields, remained outside.

Then it sank its liquid fingers into the veins of the rivers that ran under the city. It fattened the rivers until they started to bleed into the bottom of the pit. In no time at all the water had started to turn the soil to rich, sticky mud. The water began to rise.

The mud held the singers in place lovingly, easily. The water washed up over the shrine, carrying the worshipped bones and trinkets away. The singers cried out to their king – surely the time for him to return was upon them?

Sing louder – said the leader, who believed in the power of the voice above all else because he had always found using his own voice loudly to be an effective method of getting what he wanted. Everyone sang until the water slid down their throats and filled their lungs and claimed them more intimately than devotion for a king ever could.

3. Decipherings

I instruct the Gamekeeper to prepare the glider and then I fly us out over Origin. No matter how many times I visit, it continues to fascinate and impress me – a raised doughnut of a structure in the ocean, far from any reclaimed land, self-powering from the waves that beat at its angled sides, and the algae that grows in its deep tanks. I set us down on one of the many landing points that rise straight up like spines from its tubular form, and find a class of students has only just arrived on their solar bus and are waiting for the next elevator. I have no wish to cramp their style so I wait for them to board. We catch the next one so that we can be alone as we descend.

'The temple first?' I ask him, and he nods, and shifts his weight from one foot to the other. He is so excited that he trembles. I take his hand and squeeze it tight.

For my last prolonged stay I requested a deep sea-level quarter and found a new way of living, without sound, without company. It feels like a small betrayal to bring him here and talk to him, soothe him, but I like the niggling guilt; it suggests I might be growing out of the ideals I had held dear at that time.

Down we go, down through the water, and Origin's gamekeeper reports softly that it's a clear day without alerts. It makes its careful adjustments to the atmosphere to keep us comfortable.

'What made you so certain that this was the right place to dig?' he asks.

'You've researched my story, haven't you? You already know that answer,' I say, amused.

'But I like to hear you talk of it.'

So I tell him, and halfway through my tale we come to rest at Temple Level. We look out through the clear wall at the smooth white and gold stones that were once placed so carefully here by the bare calloused hands of those who worked for an idea beyond survival. What did they want? Whom did they praise? I have spent so much of my life looking through what's left of the time before the world was underwater. I have pieced together my theories, and tried to find how we have all come from the same fears and hopes. Past, present, and future humans – will we always have that need for it to be about more than simply living? Even now, when life can be extended for so long, we are not free of the search for meanings.

I finish my recollection without really having heard a word I've said. How strange, to have talked in that way. Without interest in my own voice.

It seems he was not listening either. 'Can I touch you?' he asks.

'Here?'

'Yes, why not?'

I agree. Why not make love in the very place where I first discovered my love of deep solitude, and then fell out of its grace? Time will move on but I'll have this moment.

Usually he wants us to lie together in the dark. Often we snuggle under piles of blankets like animals in a den, but in the dim lights of the elevator he takes time to look at me. I have such wrinkles. Chasms and crevices. He runs his fingers over them while I smooth a path along his body, from limb to fine limb. Do I want to be young again? To unlearn, so I could fill myself up afresh?

We stay naked, and sit together on the floor of the elevator for a while. But eventually his stomach rumbles, and we get dressed, and instruct the Gamekeeper to ascend.

'It's the most wonderful thing I've ever seen,' he says. 'They prayed here. They lived lives of such power. Can we go and see the Upraised Boy now?'

'He's in the main body of the museum. Waiting for you.'

'You want to know why I've never been to see him before?' He hesitates, swallows. 'I was afraid to see it through my own eyes. I thought it might look stupid to me. If I saw it on my own. But with you, here, I can see it properly. With the respect it deserves. As an important part of a wonderful place. Origin is so much more than I could have hoped for. I was so worried that all I might see was some stories in the mud. Thank you for giving me better vision than that.'

Some stories in the mud.

It's a phrase that sticks.

I try not to think about those words in the months of our relationship that follow, but they sink in. They are like the shiny things and the bones that are all that remain after the water rises with ferocity. And I've learned that the water always rises.

Pre-Climate Adaptation Cataclysms: The Sun

After the sea retreated nobody in the pit was left alive. Almost nobody. When the farmers came to Empty Earth to check why their loved ones had not come back from worship they found a lone infant, a chubby baby trapped in a vast lake of mud, screaming as loudly as anyone had ever screamed. It was rescued by the brave farmers who formed a human chain across the mud to reach it, mainly just to stop it from making such an awful sound, which just goes to show that the leader had been right about the power of the voice.

The baby was raised by the farmers. Fed and clothed and loved. The farmers decided some great goodness must have passed into the infant to keep it safe. With that sort of sentiment surrounding it the baby soon grew into more of a symbol than a human being, and by the time it was a child it had become the ultimate symbol: a king.

The idea that the child was the old king (who had been an emperor) reborn came easily to the farmers. It felt gratifying and made sense of their own experiences of life: the constant growing and dying back. The child was told it was an ancient and wonderful being in the grip of eternal renewal and liked that idea a lot. It grew up to believe it was the centre of everything – the past, present and future of the city embodied.

Soon after that the child began to make its own proclamations. It announced it didn't want to be called a king at all. It was the city, so that was the name that would suit it best.

I'm City – it said, and the farmers agreed, and bowed low before it.

At that point City decided that milk should no longer be the only thing in its diet, and it set out into the well-kept fields to try the produce that grew there. The tastes of the carrots and potatoes were overwhelming. It loved to bite and chew and savour, but once it had tasted everything that grew in the fields it craved different culinary experiences.

More – it said. *City more.*

Go find – it said. *Find more.*

The farmers understood. City wanted the boundaries of its life to expand with the boundaries of its stomach. So they chose those with the youngest, fastest legs to go out into the world and try to find new fruits. These messengers were ordered forth, down the old roads that had long since fallen into disrepair. They were told to travel day and night, with no thought of rest, to satisfy the hunger of City.

While the messengers travelled, City grew tired of the piles of traditional crops that were being carefully stockpiled, as was the farmers' habit. It made a face until the farmers took the crops away and threw them in the swamp of Empty Earth. This made City laugh and clap its hands together, and so the throwing of the crops became a daily occurrence without which City would not take his nap.

Once City had grown up to the point of no longer finding the crop-throwing so amusing it was also thrown into the swamp, and a new baby was found to be City. It seemed obvious to everyone involved that City needed to be a child.

Life and death went on, for a time.

The sea and the land liked this business of crop-throwing and body-throwing. The swamp was the place in which sea and land combined and mingled to become one. The receiving of the crops felt like an offering to them both.

But the sun had a temper when provoked, and it felt insulted by the wasting of crops it had commanded to grow. Its rage built until it decided to make its anger known by beating down with particular ferocity; the plants shrivelled and the rivers dried up and the people wilted and the swamp set hard. The sun wanted all things to die in order so that they could understand its power, if only for the moment before they knew no more.

City hated the heat. It stood in the centre of the swamp, lifted up its arms and commanded the sun to stop. So the sun beat down with all its rage upon such foolishness until City became a desiccated shell with lips pulled back and hair no more than an old man's wisps from a once fine mane. Then the sun felt satisfied and dimmed itself to a more sedate setting.

4. Sacrifices.

'You believe in pain?' I ask him. 'Is that what your theory comes down to – pain holding importance beyond its role in our survival mechanisms?'

The hall is crowded; the post-Celebrate 14527 party is in full swing, and he is one of the main attractions. I shouldn't even be starting this conversation now.

I find myself thinking of the first time I suspected he was looking for something in history, in the act of interpretation, with which I would profoundly disagree. It was when he gazed upon the Upraised Boy, and copied its famous stance, head thrown back, placating the heavens. *I praise the sun and sea* – he said to me – *so that, someday, they might take me.*

I have long loved that statue. It formed the crux of my first theories of ancient urban life. I did not think of it as a celebration of sacrifice but as a warning of disasters befallen. A marker, too. A remembrance. And so I chose to dig the spot upon which I found it, back before the modern craze for my subject existed. I was thought of as a little strange, to say the least. Nobody wanted to be reminded of the many dystopic ages that preceded us: the population booms, the cycles of growth and starvation, the inequality and the ignorance. But my interest in such things was tolerated by the older generation because they knew of the importance of allowing each generation to set their own agenda – as I must tolerate my young lover now.

'That's not it at all,' he says, in response to my question, frowning. 'That's not it. But I ask – what did they gain from their suffering? By extension – what do we lose by choosing to remove it?'

'The notion of choice in the act of escaping pain disturbs me greatly,' I admit. 'Surely it's one of the human constants?'

He can bear my presence, my questions, no longer. Not when the rest of the room would praise him. 'I'm so sorry to have disturbed you,' he hisses. 'Oh wondrous sage.' He walks away and mingles with others, their enthusiasm for his ideas clearly written on their faces. I would guess they're all about the same age: ageless, as they would have it.

Nobody comes to talk to me. Perhaps they're remembering my reputation as a hermit. I used to like being famous for being alone. Now I simply feel vulnerable.

I can't leave the party. It would be noted, seen as a sign of my disapproval of his presentation. It might affect his career. I can't do that to him even though his latest theories appal me. I stay, holding a flute of champagne and hoping to look over and catch him mirroring me. But he's not drinking at all. He's too busy talking, holding court. He is the centre of the room tonight, wherever he stands, and he loves it. I know exactly what he's feeling.

I could throw myself back into work. I could dig deeper and further.

No. No, my interest in it all is waning again. He gave it back to me for a while, but now it's leaving me. As he has left me.

The party is emptying, and he's not here any more. I would have liked a goodbye, but I suppose I always did suspect that the end would come suddenly, and I'm not sorry. Better this than to stare at the encroaching disaster until my eyes are sore from the sight of it.

I make up my mind to retreat. The forest calls. Let it comfort me, and I'll make it all my own again.

Pre-Climate Adaptation Cataclysms: The Wind

The sea took the opportunity to send up moisture to the sky, forming fresh white clouds that rained on the fields to start the cycle of life again. By the time the latest set of messengers returned there was plentiful food to be picked. But their family and friends had turned to dust and City itself had been mummified, preserved, standing with its arms raised high above its head.

The messengers fell down before City and dropped their armfuls of foreign fruits and prickly seeds before him. They wept, and their tears fell on their bounty. How would they manage alone, with no child to guide them? Who would be their symbol now?

It took them a few months of crying to work out that City being dead did not stop it from being an excellent symbol. In fact, life was easier. They no longer had to listen to City's babbling or obey its commands to go travelling. The seeds they had brought back had sprouted in the newly fertile land of Empty Earth, fed by their tears and the long-forgotten bodies of their ancestors trapped down in the temple. The new plants grew up and over the figure of City, higher than its outstretched arms, and created a bountiful place that they called Paradise.

The messengers became the gardeners of Paradise, tending the plants, weaving clothes and headdresses for each other, taking care of the insects and animals that came to live within. How rich Paradise was! The gardeners walked amongst the scents and sounds, rich white blooms and buzzing hearts, and breathed deeply. They had never been so happy, and that happiness lasted as they bred and tended, content.

A merely pleasant city can be held as home by those who are prepared to overlook its problems, but a paradise is a different thing altogether. Paradise only had one problem, but it became all-consuming to the Gardeners over the years because they had no other problems with which to compare it. It was the issue of the wind.

The wind would huff out its giant breaths and scatter the carefully cultivated seeds of the plants of Paradise wherever it liked, spreading weeds and creating its own wild hybrids that grew coarse, ugly and vital. They asked the wind to stop but it did not listen so they turned to City once more, searching for the mummified remains at the centre of Empty Earth. It had been entirely covered by a tenacious, clinging plant unlike any they had seen before; it grew fast and high and it allowed moisture and sunshine to slide through its gaps but kept the wind from entry with its cleverly elongated leaves that locked together.

It was the solution they had been looking for. They took cuttings from the plant and grew it up over a vast wooden frame they constructed around Empty Earth. The sun and the rain and even the land had no issue with this turn of events but the wind was very unhappy, for it was a social wind that liked nothing more than to touch. It had enjoyed stroking hair and brushing over backs, and it had liked to make the plants dance along with its good moods. All that had been taken away.

Loneliness sank in and changed it. It became low and mean, but it could not break through the wall of plants. Then it became barely able to stir, and nobody noticed its apathy. And then it gave up altogether, and left.

But the wind was not just wind. It was the air itself: moving air, turning air, air at play. Without wind, nothing could live. Not the animals, not the insects, not the plants. Not the gardeners who had been messengers who had been farmers who had been singers who had been essential workers who had survived all forms of city life for so very long. They sank down on their knees in Paradise, clutching at their throats, clawing at their mouths, their chests heaving, their eyes popping, until they all came to an abrupt end.

The mummified symbol of City ossified. It stayed tall in the centre of Empty Earth, stone and strong, a child with its face turned up to the sun, its feet planted in the land, its young slender back to the sea.

Eventually the sun and sea and land forgot all that had happened, and so did the wind, which wandered back, and all four of them stared at the statue. They remembered the days of the creatures that had amused and angered them.

Let's do it again – said sun, and the others agreed. New people arrived at the old place, found all to be pleasant and calm, and built a settlement that became a town that then swelled to a city.

5. Prayers

The Gamekeeper chimes a high alert; my wrist throbs with it.

It's him, I think. He's come back. I've wanted that scenario to play out so badly over these past weeks. It takes me precious time to work out that's not the reason for the alert at all.

A storm is forming. A class forty-three. I should return to the safest part of the forest, the sleeping area that has been dug down into the ground. Out here, in my cultivated garden, the defences aren't quite so reliable. It's an older model of climate protective device. An old thing, like me.

I sit amongst the ears of wheat.

The Gamekeeper chimes again, then starts to close up the outer shell. I watch it form, the organic materials weaving into a strong cage surrounding the Forest. This is not my field of expertise by any means, and I don't understand how it works. I've always found it an impressive sight. I even watched it from above, once, on a glider that was racing ahead of the storm to reach safety. I saw hundreds of such domes being knitted over the land. I've never forgotten my awe.

By now I should be inside.

Why did I want the Gamekeeper's chime to be about him? Have I missed him so much? Yes, I have, but I have to admit to myself that part of what I wanted was the story of his return to me. A romance. A circular construction, not unlike a recreation of ancient worship. With that realisation comes the knowledge that he is not entirely wrong when he talks about pain as a driving force. We make stories from pain. Justifications, explanations. I make no story for the wind because it has not been given the opportunity to hurt me. Until now.

The storm is upon my defences. It roars and throws itself against the structure. I wait to find out if the materials will hold. Do I still have faith in such protections?

What do we lose by choosing to remove suffering?

Only someone who has never really suffered could ask such a question, but the act of pointing this out feels wrong to me. It's not my work to dig up the future.

The wind is alive and so strong. I flinch before it, and say under my breath:

Please, not me. Not me, not now. I beg you.

Even though I'm very old and I don't understand what's coming next, I still want to live. The storm is ongoing.

A Million Moving Parts

The words stopped working on a Tuesday afternoon in the early autumn, during the hour of the television quiz show. The contestants stood, side by side, on their podiums and said things. They could be heard. Alicia was certain she was hearing them. Whether they were giving answers to question asked, she couldn't tell.

Alicia changed channel to the news. The presenter was open-mouthed. His hands trembled. He adjusted the collar of his shirt and swallowed. The camera cut to a holding scene of swirling colours.

She had once been muscled and slim with brown hair she wore long and a liking for sunshine. They lived close to the beach. Not the busy end, where the tourists packed themselves in tight, one family every four yards – why did they do that, when only half a mile up there was so much space? An expanse of fine sand, unmeasurable, blown free of footprints over and over again. She'd always been glad of the laziness of others. She had run the beach in the early morning for thirty years, until a torn ligament hadn't healed well, and she had decided to lapse into lie-ins that turned into an acceptance of old age, and muscles that didn't want to move.

Travis came and sat beside her on the sofa. Alicia pressed the mute button on the remote control and few times. On, off, on off. She said, '   '
'   ' he said.

He had watched the process of aging take hold of his wife with regret, with annoyance. If she was old, so was he. But he did not blame her. He hated confrontation, and throughout their marriage Alicia had been accommodated as much as loved, given everything, supported, and bolstered and coddled. Travis had a warm, soft body that he loved to wrap around her; he was meant to be the soft to Alicia's hard, but she drooped, she spread, and it now made him a little queasy to touch her, like eating too many marshmallows. Where had his hard warrior gone? Who protected him now?

'   ' she said.

'   '

'   '

She changed channels, and the rerun of a sitcom popped up. Not soundless, exactly. The actors were speaking. Alicia knew this episode, and could quote a line or two.

In her forties, Alicia had joined a climbing club and found herself spending time with an instructor called Maggie, years younger, with no fear in her. They had gone on a weekend away to a place in the Wye Valley, and Maggie had encouraged her to try harder and harder routes. Alicia had been unable to keep fear out of her voice as they discussed approaches to the grainy cliff faces. When it came to the most difficult climbs, she often balked. She'd felt such shame about being unable to control herself. It had not been the height that scared her. She loved the feel of the rocks under her fingers, either solid or shifting objects at the moment of connection. And she hadn't been scared of the idea of having an affair; she had fantasised about Maggie often, but knew she would never do such a thing to Travis.

It was Maggie herself who was frightening. Maggie was a conqueror in some great epic, striding continents in her Lycra shorts and singlet. She had taken a job as an outward-bound instructor up north and never returned, never left a way to find her. Sometimes Alicia got the urge to type her name into the phone, maybe find a social media profile with a photo of Maggie now. But what good would it do her to see that colossus compromised by time? She resisted. There was a time when Maggie had led the way, high up the cliff face, Alicia below, attempting to keep up. And Maggie had turned her head and shouted down, the vibrations travelling through the rope that joined them together. Words caught by the gusting wind, bouncing off the rocks, never reaching her ears. Alicia wondered, now, why she had found that all so scary when it had become one of her favourite memories. The colours on the screen swirled on.

'   ' said Travis.

Alicia shook her head. She stood, felt the usual twinge ache in her lower back, and went to the front door. She opened it wide, her toes on the threshold of the welcome mat, and listened.

Travis came up behind her, leaned in close.

'   '

'   '

Their house was small but detached, an older build that had been incorporated into a new estate when land was sold around them. This coastal town had grown so large. There was only one main road that permanently needed repairs, yet still the council made plans to try to find spaces for more houses. How many could be squeezed onto finite land? Only the farmer who owned the field to the west was keeping expansion at bay.

On certain days, the wind arriving from inland, the traffic could be clearly heard as a busy stream of sound. If the wind blew in from the beach instead, there was the hush of the sea. It could be easy to confuse one with the other, sometimes. That day it was the sea that won out: rhythmic, soothing. Travis and Alicia listened to it. Their ears were definitely not broken. The sea, at least, was unchanged.

Travis grabbed the house keys from the bowl in the hallway, and they stepped into the street. He closed the door gently behind them. They walked around the bend that led to their cul-de-sac and saw the rest of the road laid out before them like a long table laid for a meal, everything just so, the new-build houses in place, the glass shining. The window cleaner had done his rounds that morning.

A boy was riding his scooter, fast, away from them. He lifted one leg in a pose as he passed the large horse chestnut on the grass verge, its candles in bloom, conkers not yet given up to gravity.

Travis loved conkers. He collected them every year from this tree and kept them in a bowl in the living room until they developed a fuzzy mould. He liked the idea they kept spiders at bay, although he didn't really believe it. He never saw any of the local children collect them, but always left a few of the biggest conkers on the grass for them, just in case.

He was the youngest of three brothers, and the other two had loved to play conkers against each other: drilling, stringing, smashing. Travis had hovered on the edge of their circle, watching the action, and they had never once asked him to play. Eventually he had said something to his mother, who had demanded his inclusion – a mistake, he knew, a sign of weakness – and they had given him a strung conker of his own, then taken turns missing it and cracking their own polished specimens down on his knuckles. He'd borne it as punishment for as long as he could, then run back into the house and watched them from the upstairs window instead.

The conker phase fizzled out for his brothers soon after that, and they found new games to play. Sometimes he was included, sometimes not. When his own son came along, beautiful Samuel, he had stressed often that everyone should have a share in games, in joy, in life. They had not played conkers once. Samuel now worked in Europe as an investment portfolio manager. Travis reached the tree. He put his hand to it, felt the strong pattern of the bark on the trunk.

'   ' he said, more to himself than to Alicia. The kid on the scooter turned the last corner before the main road, and was out of sight.

Travis phoned Samuel when they got back in. The line connected, and Travis made shapes with his mouth, then passed the phone to Alicia, who did the same before hanging up. They could picture Samuel doing the same thing. It was a comfort.

The oven timer pinged. Dinner was chilli con carne, made to a recipe that had started out as Alicia's mother's invention. Since then it had been tweaked often enough to qualify as Alicia's own, with the addition of home-grown chilli from the greenhouse, a little streaky bacon, and a square of cooking chocolate dropped into the centre of the thick tomato and mince mess before the lid of the casserole was put in place, and the whole thing left to unctuate for three hours or longer. Spooned into bowls, served with flatbreads for dipping, it was one of Alicia's favourite meals. Her tongue and teeth worked, and her throat swallowed. Every part of her mouth was capable, up to the job.

Travis grated cheese on his portion and stirred it in. He ate at speed, as he always did when worried. When she cleared his bowl away, she patted his shoulder, and he reached up to squeeze her hand.

He took her hand again when they sat down on the sofa and stroked her knuckles with his thumb. The television showed more newsreaders looking lost, eyes shifting as if there was too much before them to take in. Occasionally letters flashed onscreen; at least, Travis thought they were letters. They were grouped together oddly.

Lying in bed that night, Alicia thought back and decided the words had been ill for a long time. A process of denuding had been taking place around her, and not only since her retirement. Before then, in the office or out on calls, she had seen the words rushing away as if thrown into a fast-moving river. She thought of conversations she'd had and speeches she'd listened to, when the rhythm had overcome her and she'd been lulled, almost anaesthetised, only to jerk back to the present and realise she'd taken in nothing. Hadn't she done that with Samuel, too, when he was little? Barely managed to really communicate with him at all. She lay still, in guilt. She'd been complicit.

Travis turned over, careful not to take the duvet with him. Alicia was a light sleeper, and he didn't want to disturb her. She was prone to getting cold now she no longer exercised regularly, and it could lead to cramp. He couldn't count the number of times he had ended up massaging her calves at three in the morning, all the lights of the town off, kneading out knots in the dark. The way she breathed, then, was different to any sound he heard her make during the day. She took shallow, coarse breaths that eventually eased back into sleep. In the mornings she rarely remembered she'd been in such pain. It reminded him of when she'd given birth and he had rubbed her back, felt the pain move through her, rise to his palms. He had felt important, instrumental in the event: a fantasy, maybe. She did not remember it the same way at all, and when they talked of it she often said it had barely hurt.

It was the strangest thing, to remember an event so differently, but he did not feel that difference diminished its importance. Surely the bigger the happening, the more ways there should be to think of it? Like now, like the suffering of the words leading to this death, and the part they all had played in travelling to that destination. How come Alicia was suddenly a deep sleeper, this night above all others? She should have been awake. He pulled the duvet from her. She said, '   ', and he realised she had been lying awake beside him the entire time, after all.

The television was showing a silent film again.

The more Alicia watched these films, the more beauty she saw in the past – not her own, but the world as it was before she was born into it. There was a simplicity to everything that she had complicated with her thoughts, her feelings. The more she tried to interpret her place in it all, the more complex she made it.

The handsome actor was on his knees, hands clutched to his chest, expression anguished. Before him, half-turned to the camera, was a woman in a long dress. She sat on a chaise longue, slippers poking out from under the hem. Her face was composed; how could she be so still, faintly smiling, while he suffered? It was as if his pain fed her pleasure. A caption card flashed onscreen. Letters. Curves and sticks at irregular intervals. The inexplicable scene returned. Alicia left it playing and went in search of Travis.

He was at the bottom of the garden, in the greenhouse. It always looked as if it was at the moment of collapse, but it never did fall. Travis worried about it. He had gone through a phase of placing and adjusting breezeblocks around it, and stringing twine over its pointed roof. Alicia stopped outside the door and watched him clean the panes with a damp rag. The orange bucket from under the sink sat beside his feet; no doubt he'd filled it with warm soapy water for the task. Soon the rag would be dirtied and the salt crystals on the panes would smear. Then he would dip it into the bucket, wring it out, and start again. She rarely interrupted him when he took up this task, but as the days of wordlessness dragged on she felt less capable of sticking to their old routines. She did not want the comfort they offered.

She stepped around the side of the greenhouse, so she was in his line of sight, and tapped the glass. He stopped rubbing with the rag and they looked at each other, with a clarity that should have been eroded by time spent together. Dispassionate, objective. Faces bare. What did they see? Her own face couldn't be controlled. It contorted, her lips pulling back. Terror took her. Nothing could ever be controlled.

Travis dropped the rag and emerged from the greenhouse, pushing through the low-hanging strands of the grapevine and bushy chilli plants in their pots, to hold her. He felt the familiar angles of her fear. It had always been a part of her, this sudden jerking into panic, but every time it came back she treated it as a new foe that needed defeating. It would take an age to calm her down. Usually he would have spoken of certain things, of times past, and lead her into remembrance where everything was safe and neatly sorted, but in the absence of that he led her back indoors and made tea, and hoped that would take her back to all the times he had made her mint tea just as she liked it, with half hot and half cold water so it was easy to drink.

He had no taste for mint tea himself, did not care for hot drinks in the main. Lately he'd started to feel surprised every time he switched on the kettle for her to find it still working. Why should some things continue to function when the biggest thing, the words themselves, did not? How long could this go on? He'd found, in these thoughts, a hard core within his softness. He had begun to make plans for making sure neither of them suffered.

A friend who moved overseas, oh, years ago, had given his affection to a dog. They had been inseparable. Man and dog. The dog had looked at the man with such adoration, attention never wavering except in sleep, and it had been trained to do tricks when it heard certain words. Travis had wondered what the dog was hearing when the words were uttered. A meaning? A command? A sound accompanied by a way of looking, of acting, that demanded a certain response? His friend had told him it was all in the way the word was said.

The dog developed cancer and needed to be put to sleep. After the event, he had sat with his friend in a coffee shop for hours. They had not spoken. What words had his friend spoken to the dog at the moment of death? A command to sleep? Good boys and goodbyes.

Then they had waved to each other in the terminal, before his friend flew to Costa Rica to work for a charity preserving the forest. A few phone calls, a Christmas card or two, and the friendship had petered out. No command had been needed to stop, just a mutual decision to no longer be in touch, but he hoped the man still thought of him as a friend, whatever that meant. Yes. As a friend.

Travis thought about the soapy rag, lying in the greenhouse, on the floor. Of tasks that did not end that all had to end sometime.

Was that a knock at the door?

Alicia stood up first, tea half-drunk; she was too fast for Travis. She reached the door and flung it open. It banged against the wall: a loud sound. The sunshine was bright, had broken through the clouds. There was nobody there. But there were people in the street, walking to the privet bushes at the end of the road, where there was a small dirt path created by those pushing their way through to make a short cut to the beach. The farmer who owned the field grew corn, for animal consumption, and it was possible to skirt the crop to reach a good view down to the beach. She recognised the people passing by the house, walking in groups of twos or threes, sometimes more: her neighbours. They were strolling, in the main. Some of the children were running and making noises. Calling to each other, using sounds that were approaching meaning once more. Maybe the words would come back, for them, she thought, and was filled with the need to phone Samuel again. She left the door open, pushed past Travis, and snatched up the receiver. There was no dialling tone. Pressing the button didn't change that, so there was nothing to do but replace it on the cradle.

She returned to the door.

Maybe a neighbour had knocked and moved on down the street. There were more people now, from further afield. She recognised the woman who worked at the local supermarket, seemingly behind the till at all hours, glum since the arrival of self-service. Occasionally Alicia had queued with her small basket of expensive essentials just to let the woman beep them through, and then had requested a scratch card just for the sake of the interaction, never expecting to win anything. She did not really believe in luck, but when it had come to her with a win of five hundred pounds, revealed through the slick layer of silver over the cardboard, she had felt vindicated in her support of the woman, who now smiled at her as she moved along down the road, and disappeared through the gap in the hedges.

People moving together, single units coagulating: there was something powerful about it. The sound today was not of the sea, but the road, and it was busy. Alicia could picture all the cars and trucks and campervans and motorbikes and articulated lorries streaming onwards, downwards, to destinations. The terror returned with the thought that the sea might not be there any more, taken away as suddenly as the words – once she had thought it, it could not be banished – and she surprised herself by making a sound, a kind of grunt, that Travis responded to. He grabbed the keys from the basket by the door, and they both stepped into the street once more, into the sunshine, falling into the flow of bodies, making their way through the gap to find the field of corn had been shorn, the long tall sheaves cut down for storage, and only stubbled, ripped roots remained. People were not keeping to the side of the field but fanning out across it, taking up space, transforming it into a crowded gathering, but they still all moved towards the view, and Alicia and Travis found themselves at the crest of that rise, looking down over the sea, still there, the tide going out, the wet shiny expanse of the sand revealed.

'   ' Alicia said, and Travis nodded.

The beach was filling up. Not just the busy end, nearer the town, but the whole length of it, people sitting and standing and some dancing, turning cartwheels. The urge to run overcame Alicia and she caught Travis's sleeve and pulled him forwards, stumbling over the lip of the hill and down the dune, the finer sand grabbing at their feet. It didn't matter that they were old and tired. They threaded their way through the gathering, down towards the open water as it retreated from them, half-expecting to never reach it, and the sand turned wet, wetter, until their feet began to sink into the million moving parts that made up the beach, leaving the perfect imprints of their sodden shoes, showing precisely where they had been and where they were going.

Streamers

Alight with movement, we travel.

We were fixed on the goal of a global, sustainable transit system that didn't start from scratch. We had roads and cars: enough to tie the world in loops, sew it up in stitched networks. We couldn't wipe them away, so we didn't try.

It was the project of a generation: how to create a solution from the bones of the problem itself? We thought it was the last great problem of our time, and the answer came to us through the collaboration of teams working in engineering, aerodynamics, quantum mechanics, artificial intelligence, nanotechnology, plasma. We were based in Kolkata, Fudan, Cambridge, Aix-en-Provence, St Petersburg, Hanyang, Cologne. Back when cities were separate entities in our minds.

How can we put across the many barriers we overcame to find ways to work together? Time and language were our enemies. We could find no form of communication that did not involve a loss of meaning or ability in some way. If we worked in one language and time zone, the others were disadvantaged. Off-world facilities were far too expensive to justify at the time when we were still in the process of undoing historic injustices of wealth imbalance. We battled on, relying on translation, sharing physical space when we could.

The breakthroughs were not moments of genius. They were small happenings, inches gained. Then we looked back, and saw how far we'd come, and the prototype streamer was completed without the realisation that it was all we needed, and more. Wasn't it only a row of modified cars? Wasn't it simply a smart road with additional features?

Travel is adaptation. We move on, and move on, and adaptation is the greatest part of us. It is what has made us human, and now makes us more. Every action was seen as a singular step on a long road, but the answer to that last great problem lay in no longer viewing our achievements that way at all.

There are enough vehicles in the world; what is the benefit of pretending each is an island of autonomy? Every journey is shaped by the path laid out before it, shared with others on the same route. Our roads converge, cross, sometimes stymying the plans of the traveller. The only solution was to give up on the illusion of choice, and there it was: the car, not as a unit of travel, but as a shared purpose in itself. No A to B. No place that's better to be than another. That's what we needed to create.

A description:

The first car heads the streamer and steers the way. It uses resources, yes, but the heat from the exhaust is converted using thermoelectrics, recharging the batteries – not of itself, but of the car behind, tethered to it, aligned by the AI network, and then connected via repurposed mid-travel aviation refuelling techniques. A third car attaches. A fourth. Ten. Fifty. The system is refined, the mechanisms improved. Excess thermoelectricity is fed into the smart road itself, and one car can now fuel a thousand. Thousands.

It changed more than the car itself. People began to wonder why they sat alone in their tethered boxes. They began to unite in their streams. Then offline. What used to be a car boot became a doorway. The streams began to include food, entertainment, companionship. People joined and left for what they needed. The mode of travel became the destination.

To the present day. Travellers never leave the stream. Why would they? Travel is adaptation, and we are on a different kind of journey now, together, where an end point has ceased to exist in physical form. The latest development is the fitting of a laser to the roof of each vehicle, attached to the AI system. It controls what colours are shown, and when, creating beautiful effects, long threads, steady or flickering. The results are visible from space. The Earth itself has become a canvas upon which we paint, and the message of the artform is: we are together. We are joined. Is this the first language we all truly speak?

The light itself is travelling, out into space. Maybe, in the future, it will reach others. Our planet, visibly transmitting.

Here is what we have learned from our journey:

There is no last great problem of any age. We have run out of room for roads that run along the ground. The new problem, for the generations beyond us, is how to take our lights to further worlds, how to reach those who live there. A truly universal, sustainable transit system. Time and language will be the enemies of those who take up this challenge. They will find out who, or what, will be their friends.

But for now, alight with movement, flooded in change, we travel. We have always been travelling.

Pack Your Coat

It swept through our school at a ferocious rate. By the time first bell had sounded for break everyone already knew it, and it was busily mutating in the playground to appeal even more to the children that shared it.

Such stories are viruses. They have a life of their own. They breathe, and move, and infect us.

This one was about an orange coat.

I didn't realise how much it had a hold on me until I came across it again, twenty years later, in my office.

'My sister's friend,' said Katie.

'Your sister's friend saw him?' Tyler leaned forward, over his desk, his attention fully diverted from his computer.

'What's this?' I said. I'd just finished a call with a potential buyer for the business. It was the first sniff in an age, and I had been indulging myself in the dream of leaving town for good, starting over somewhere else, as I emerged from the back room to get a coffee.

'Tell her,' said Tyler. 'Start at the beginning.'

She walks along the top of the cliffs, with eyes cast down, attention reserved only for the sea. It is unpredictable where the rocks jut out; the waves bulge and then spray erupts over the jagged peaks. But this is all happening far below her, and there is no path down. The cliffs have been marked as unsafe, and wire nets have been stapled over the barefaced slabs that threaten to fall. It feels like containment to her; if they should crash, let them go.

There isn't much daylight left. The tide is coming in fast. The waves have a ferocity to them that excites her. Soon the rocks will be covered, and then the small lip of the beach below.

The dog is having a fine time, capering ahead of her, stopping, sniffing, running on. She doesn't call him back. He'll come when he's ready.

The path diverges from the cliff, turning inwards, and gorse bushes spring up on either side, but she ignores it and sticks to the edge instead. It's her usual route. A faint track has established itself through footfall over the years. She's not sure whether it's been made only by her own walking, or if she's just one of many locals who come this way.

The wind shifts direction to blow her hair straight back, bringing tears to her eyes and new sounds to her ears. Seagulls. The shush and crash of water. The dog, barking.

She calls for him, and he doesn't come.

She speeds up, scanning for him, and finally spots him in the distance. He's very close to the edge, dodging forwards, barking, chasing around in a circle to start again. Shouting at him does no good. She runs the remaining distance, the cold wind stabbing at her face, into her lungs, and grabs his collar to clip on the lead.

His attention is still on the edge. She looks over and sees, on the rocks, an orange coat.

It takes her a moment to work out that it's not just a coat, flapping. A man wears it. He is waving.

She waves back. He does not stop waving, using both arms over his head. The spray of the waves is soaking him in regular bursts. He slips to one knee, then struggles to stand.

There's no boat, no sign of how he got there. Did he climb down? How can he climb back up?

The waves are breaking so close to him. For a moment he is hidden from view by a fierce uprush of the sea, and she holds her breath. But he's still there when it recedes. He is looking at her.

She takes out her phone and dials the emergency number. She asks for the coastguard and describes where he is. She feels calm, even though the dog is pulling at the lead, still barking. She can't hear what the voice is saying. 'What was that?' she asks.

'Hold on,' says the voice. 'Hold on.' It's not really a message for her, but for the man on the rocks, so she shouts it down to him, knowing that he can't possibly hear her.

He continues to wave. She can't wave back any more, with one hand holding the lead and the other holding the phone. 'Hold on,' she calls again.

She feels the big wave coming. There's a pattern to the sea. The smaller waves clashing over the rocks can only lead to a larger swell. The sea pulls back, exposing more of the rock on which he stands, and then the water surges over him entirely, like a sheet being thrown into the air to settle on a bed.

When it recedes, he's gone.

She scans for a sign of him. The orange coat. Surely that will be visible? Her eyes will find the orange coat. But she does not see it, and the coastguard does not find it, even though they search for hours, well into the night.

Later on, an official suggests delicately to her that maybe the man was a product of her imagination. Not there at all.

'That's an old one,' I say. It has made some more changes to itself since the first time I heard it, but I'd know it anywhere. It's the coat that gives it away; the coat is always the same.

'It just happened last week,' says Katie. 'To my sister's friend.'

'Friend of a friend of a friend,' adds Tyler, and smiles at me.

I try to think of something managerial to say, but the best I can come up with is some old cliché about time being money, and then I retreat to my office, abandoning my plans for coffee in my desire to get away from the same old conversations, the usual crowd. The story that never ends.

I meet Sarah in the Ship and Anchor. She's already ordered two white wines. Large ones. It's been a bad week for her too, then.

We sit in the back room. It was once called the Ladies' Lounge, and is always quieter than the main bar, as if memories of those times continue to permeate the atmosphere.

'Here's to Fridays.'

'Fridays,' I echo. She starts talking, and I listen. She's not from here originally, so even when she's moaning about life, I find it more bearable than talking to the people I grew up amongst. She brings a fresh perspective to it all, which makes me feel better for a while.

I tell her about the possible buyer for the firm.

'That's brilliant! I know it's taken a while, but I've always said someone was going to come along. That place is a goldmine. Solar panels are the future.'

'Not my future, hopefully.'

She knows this story too. I inherited a business from my father, gave it a few tweaks to bring it up to the present day, and have been tied to it ever since. And she's wrong: it's not a goldmine. It's a life support machine. It sustains me and ties me to itself. Being connected to it, and this town, is almost like living, and nothing like a life at all.

'Are they offering enough?' says Sarah.

'Just about.' I have a whole year of travel planned. I've had my route marked on a map above my bed for years. I used to trace it with my finger. 'There's a long way to go yet, though.'

She doesn't say *good luck* or *fingers crossed* or anything along those lines, which is another reason why I like her. She tips her glass to touch mine, and we both drink.

'Why do you hate this town so much?' she asks. 'It's really not so bad. There are worse places to live.'

This is something I've never explained to her, no matter how many times she asks the question. I suspect she'd think me crazy if I told her that it is the act of belonging here that makes me hate it. It claims me as its property, and the more I struggle, the more it presents reasons to stay. Financial, emotional. The business, my mother. Love, fear. So many things that it should not be possible to leave behind, and I resent every one of them. Fear – that's the one I hate the most.

So, I shrug and say, 'All I want is the opportunity to find that out for myself.'

'Listen,' she says. 'The strangest thing happened to my neighbour's uncle when he was walking the coastal path a while back. Apparently –'

Up high, walking free: it's the daily routine. A stroll along the cliffs. Every day the hills to the path get harder to climb, but he has it in his head now: miss a day and that's the start of the end. He's become attached to routines, that's how he phrases it to the cleaner who comes in twice a week, paid for by his nephew, who's a good lad.

Lad. He's in his forties, with children of his own, but the passage of time never quite seems to take. It's like this walk. He's done it so many times, and it's new to him every day.

The sea is unique, of course, so perhaps that's the reason. What's that quote? About never being able to stand in the same river twice. Down below, at the base of the cliffs, the sea is alive, twisting and dragging, rumbling over the spit of rocks that stretches out to form part of the natural harbour of the town. The tide is rushing in, along with the stronger light of late morning. Unstoppable.

He ignores the official path and follows the lighter trail for local feet, hugging the cliff edge. There's talk of it being dangerous, but if he's going to go in a rock fall then so be it. Nature itself, snatching away the ground from under you; you can't argue with that.

There's a girl on the rocks.

That can't be right. There's no path that leads down that way, never has been. But there she is, clear as day, in an orange coat with the hood up and her brown hair spilling out around the sides. The white spray is fierce about her as the waves dance. She has her legs planted wide, no doubt to try to keep her balance, but they are such very thin legs, sticking out from the frill of a dark dress, just visible beneath the coat.

She is waving to him.

He waves back.

She's in danger. Can't she see it? Maybe she could swim for it. Her face is very small, and his eyesight is not what it used to be, but he thinks she's smiling.

He shouts, but his voice is snatched away by the wind. Useless. If only he had one of those phones – his nephew offered to get him one, and he said he'd never use it. What a stupid thing to say. Arrogant, really, to assume there'd never be a need for such a thing.

He shouts that he'll get help.

A big wave hits, one of those that can reach far up the cliff face and make you think it can even come over the top in the worst weather, and he steps back from the edge, and catches his breath. When he looks for her again, she's not there. No sign of her, not even a flash of that bright coat.

He looks and looks, wishing for better eyes, and eventually forces himself to look away and start a shambling pace home, to find help, to reach a phone, wishing for faster legs this time. For youth. For anything that could make a difference to the day.

'The weirdest part is, the coastguard searched for hours and –'

'Didn't find a thing?' I supply smoothly.

'They found an orange coat. For a girl. But it was really old. An antique. They couldn't understand how it had survived for that long, and then to stay intact in the water, too...'

'That's a good twist,' I tell her.

'No, it's true! My neighbour told me directly. Seriously, he wouldn't lie.' She looks so earnest. I think she really wants to believe it.

This is how it survives. This is how it spreads.

The negotiations of the sale progress, and I try to focus on that alone, but my mind keeps returning to the first time I heard the story. I was very young; was *it* young too? I doubt it. It had a power to it, even then, that suggested a certain maturity.

I ran home after school that day and found my mother in the kitchen, as usual, looking out of the window towards the harbour. We lived high up in the hills, close to the old church building and the temporary cabins that constituted the school. Behind us a new estate was being built at a frightening speed. We were a growing town.

Multiply

The three of them stood close together, their heads bowed over the console.

6.1320279

'That's better than last time,' said Salma.

'Until it changes again,' said Mij.

Lars said, 'Screw it. It's not going to get any less broken. I don't know why we're even looking.'

The mechanical dials clicked over and rearranged themselves to a new number.

0.0000002

They held their breaths, and looked up, beyond the long desk of the console, through the observation window: deep space, an immeasurable amount of black, with dots of light from far stars scattered throughout. This was not a view looking forwards, but back, from the rear of the ship as it made its progress. There was no way to see what lay ahead. Still, they stared, as if answers about the future could lie in the past.

It was difficult to accept their blindness, Mij thought. Like walking backwards, slowly, carefully, knowing that a hard wall lay behind, to be collided with, at some point in time.

If only she knew on which occasion the counter had last been correct. It would have been something to hold on to. Mij recalled the plan she had memorised, provided by Doctor Troon: the steps to be undertaken upon arrival. No doubt Lars and Salma were doing the same thing. Surely, between the three of them, they could remember it all. But it was not a plan for travelling: it made no difference, now. The ship itself was knowledge beyond them. The console was an illusion of control, no more, to keep them calm. It had no pressable buttons. They were caretakers that had nothing to take care of. An illusion, for the benefit of passengers who weren't awake to care.

'It's broken,' she said, softly. 'It's broken.'

The dials on the counter clicked over.

48.5963413

A collective breath out.

'Screw it,' said Lars, again. Was that relief in his voice? 'Come on. Supper.'

Supper, and a round of Numbers.

The illusion of a day.

Mij did her best to maintain it: waking, eating breakfast, lunch and supper, showering, exercising, doing her tasks. The checking of the counter happened just before supper every day, and afterwards, they played Numbers. The game had evolved over the artificial months and now it was a craft in its precision. They played every night until all three of them had yawned. Yawns were contagious; if that sense of exhaustion could infect them then their chances of sleeping rather than lying awake were higher. They had decided on that together.

'Favourite sport,' said Lars. 'Sal, you're up.'

'Soccer,' said Salma.

Lars rolled his eyes. It was a safe guess, but Salma was behind on the tally, and looking to make up the number of wins.

'Ping pong,' said Mij.

'What's that?' said Salma.

'You don't know ping pong? Or – table tennis. That's the proper name. You play it on a table. With a net, and paddles.'

'Paddles, for rowing?'

Mij laughed. 'Not exactly.' She had always loved ping pong when she was little, playing it over the kitchen table with her brother and her cousins, using a net, paddles, and ball her father had found at a car boot sale. A very British experience, when such a thing had existed.

'I'll go for basketball,' said Lars. He pressed the space bar on the keyboard set into the wall, and the screen above it sprang into light blue life. It read:

PASSENGER MANIFEST
QUERY?

Lars typed each of their answers in, his fingers firm on the chunky keys, and they all watched as the results popped up in square black script.

SOCCER – 1,300,435
TABLE TENNIS – 156,127
BASKETBALL – 877,777

'You've got it,' Lars said to Salma. 'A good win.'

Mij picked up the pen and marked her tally on the wall, along from the keyboard. The three rows of lines continued to grow. They were nearly at the corner, after which they would start down towards the microwave, no doubt. Lars was in the lead.

The ship's galley was easily Mij's favourite room on board the *Arrow*. It was the only one that had been decorated to approximate any kind of homeliness, with thoughts of its small crew in mind. She gave silent thanks to the eccentric designer, whoever they had been, for the sturdy pine table and four chairs on a tiled floor in a geometric pattern, black and white. The mock-ups of the oven and the fridge didn't open, but they were a nice touch. Only the microwave worked, and the cupboard. They restocked the packets every month from the storeroom, and then took it in turns to reheat, and serve.

There were even curtains, red ones, that could be pulled over the passenger manifest screen and keyboard, so it could be imagined that a view lay just beyond them instead. The thought of it prompted Mij's suggestion for the next round. 'Place of birth,' she said.

Salma groaned. 'Again?'

'No cities this time. Towns only.'

'Define a town,' said Lars. He always did want to nail down every aspect of the challenge. He took it too seriously, and Mij had gone through a short period of intense dislike for him because of it. Now she had come to accept it as part of his personality, and reminded herself often to view it with amusement. Mostly, that approach worked. 'Pick a town, and then we'll all decide if it is one.'

'Could we not just define it in advance?'

'My round. My rules,' Mij told him.

He sighed. She got the feeling she annoyed him too. If only they could put aside conventions, niceties, and say to each other – *it's okay. Not getting along is hardly fatal. And perhaps it's even inevitable.*

'Gudhjem,' he said. 'It's in Denmark.'

'That's fine,' said Salma, 'although I wouldn't know one way or another, no? I choose Faiyum. You can find it in Egypt.'

'Both work for me,' said Mij. She tried not to think of how they were framing all of their answers in the present tense, as if these places still existed. 'I choose Newark-on-Trent. England.'

Lars nodded, then stepped back from the keyboard so she could type in all three answers.

Gudhjem – 0

Faiyum – 2

Newark-on-Trent – 3

'Nobody from Gudhjem?' asked Lars. 'I can't believe it. Nobody.'

'Maybe it's an error, like with the counter,' Mij said, then knew straight away she'd made a mistake to even suggest it. Salma's face showed it clearly – the dismay, the fear at the idea that the integrity of the manifest was compromised. They had to all believe that they were getting somewhere, fulfilling a purpose, and the sanctity of the canisters in the hold were the key to that. 'I'll mark it up,' she said. She took the pen and made the tally mark, grateful to look at the wall instead.

Three people from Newark-on-Trent, encased in the vast cargo deck, travelling with them. She wished she could wake them up, ask them if they ever went to the nearby city of Lincoln for the famous Christmas market. She had visited it once, with an old boyfriend, not unlike Lars in looks. Very tall, and almost handsome with the light behind him. There had been a vast, steep hill to walk up, old houses with squashed shop windows offering chocolate, wine, cheese, handmade shoes on either side. And then, at the top, between the remains of a castle and a towering cathedral, there had been stalls decorated with fairy lights, growing brighter in the approach of dusk. The smells. Mulled wine, sausages, roasted chestnuts. Her boyfriend had grabbed her arm and steered her through bunched crowds, complaining that it got busier every year, telling her he knew the best path to take.

She had dumped him in the new year, then gone to work on the *Arrow*. No complications, no time for towns and markets.

Three people.

She wondered if they had even been to the market. Sometimes, when you live close to beautiful things, exciting things, you don't think about them at all. They are just there, until they're not. On a whim, she returned to the keyboard and typed in an expansion directive. Three names came up. She didn't recognise any of them. Her old boyfriend, born in Newark, was not there.

Of course, he wasn't there. The chances of him being designated a person of importance would have been a million to one. Some astronomical number. He'd been studying International Politics at university – precisely the kind of area everyone would want to forget about when they reached their destination. A new start, without states and politicians. Isn't that what they were aiming for?

Lars yawned. It passed to Salma with ease; Mij faked hers. Maybe all the yawns tonight had been fake. It wouldn't have surprised her. She'd noticed Lars and Salma talked to each other less, and made an effort never to sit close together, and she got the feeling this was a show entirely for her benefit. There was something going on between them.

'Time to call it a night,' Lars said. He stood up and stretched. There was a touch of drama to the move.

'Goodnight, then,' Mij said. She left the room, walked the grey corridor to the sleeping quarters – three doors in a row, to matching rooms. A single bed, a sink, a shower. She had put up a few pictures cut from old magazines on the wall behind her pillow. *Rambler's Monthly*. She had loved to walk, to look at beauty and nature unrolling around her. Every day she walked the vast cargo deck, now, for fitness purposes. There was never anything new to see. The canisters were all alike; there were no windows to allow a view inside to see the faces of the passengers.

Were Lars and Salma sleeping together?

Mij mooted it as she took a quick shower. It seemed likely that Lars would want to find sexual release, physical comfort. Salma, though… she was so quiet, far from talkative or demonstrative. A small, watchful woman without the need for a confidante, and Mij had tried to engage her in personal conversation often, with no result. It was hard to imagine her needing human contact.

She wanted the two of them to had found love. Big, swelling, real love. A fitting start for a new beginning. Could that possibly be what was happening? As she settled herself in bed, she realised she wouldn't even know what that looked like. She had nothing inside her, no memory, to compare it with.

Mij only ever ran in a straight line.

The storage area had not been designed with ease of human navigation in mind. It consisted of suspended metal walkways in a grid layout, giving access to the canisters arranged on either side. When they arrived at their destination, the ship would open the canisters in rotating batches, brought to the main door on an overhead track system – a process that would take weeks – and only then would they have an answer to the question: how many people can be transported effectively across vast interstellar distances using cryogenic storage techniques? Maybe everyone. Maybe no one.

She ran every morning. From the moment she took the ladder down to the containment door and pressed the button to gain access to the storage deck, the vast overhead lights flickering reluctantly to life, she set her mind to the task of running with nothing to look at, no twists or turns. To take a left or right at any one of the hundreds of crossroads would have got her irrevocably lost. There were no signposts, no deviations to the rows of canisters. No need for humanity, down here.

Her mind roamed far more freely. She thought of many things, many places.

But not that morning. Instead, she found herself thinking, to the rhythm of her footfalls, of how the canisters looked like oversized silver bullets, ready to be shot against some unknown enemy. People as a weapon. It would be easy to get lost in the philosophical permutations within such a thought, but Mij tried to keep herself grounded in the reality of the situation. These were all just passengers, chosen for a place on the grounds of being the best hope for humanity, that was all. And this time they would not pollute or fight or fail to protect the systems that they needed to sustain life. They would be better than that.

I can dream, Mij thought, in time, in rhythm. *I can dream I can dream I can dream.*

And she came out of the dream and realised she had run far, and fast, and her stamina – usually so robust – was fading. She slowed, came to a stop, and breathed deeply for a while, her hands on her hips. When she turned around the containment door was no longer visible, at the end of the walkway. But of course it would be there; it was simply beyond her line of sight. She started walking back the way she had run, glad nobody was there to see her idiocy. Things didn't disappear simply because you couldn't see them, and yet it nagged at her. Had she turned off without thinking about it? Imagine being lost down here. Lost forever.

She glanced both ways at each crossroads she passed. Force of habit at this slower pace, as if she were walking down a street somewhere, intersections at which traffic might gather: an affection of Earth. How she missed it, she missed it; she tried so hard not to think about it but it had to be faced, in the sweat, in the pain of her breath. She was human, from Earth; from a depleted, useless Earth. She looked left, she looked right. Forwards.

Left. Right.

Left. Right.

Left.

She stopped walking.

To her right: something was wrong.

A shape that should not be there.

She broke her rule, and went to it. It was a dead animal, something hairless. Its limbs, jointed, a torso, a spine. Surprisingly little blood. Like a carcass in a butcher's window.

She recognised it – a sudden flash of knowledge – as human.

The head was missing. The cleanly sliced stump of the neck was angled away from her, and the arms twisted up and away, the fingers formed into claws. A violent death brought to a still frozen body.

She stepped back and crouched down. The need to get low, stay small, overwhelmed her, but also the desire to see, to be sharp, aware. She took in all the details, saw the walkway in its precision. Its angles. The row of canisters broken. The ruptured one was torn open: ragged, screwed metal compared to the clean lines of the injury on the body. How could she not have seen it before? Something had attacked the canister with ferocity, with power. It had removed the person inside, and then removed their head with such precision. From brute force to calm surgery.

The feeling of being watched overwhelmed her.

The sensation was so strong that it took control, removed the need for thought. She got up and ran, ran from the body, turned the corner and made for the cargo door at a speed she hadn't known she was capable of. Time changed. The seconds passed in a thick, slow intensity – none more so than the final moments when she reached the door and pressed the button so it swung open; allowed her to escape. She couldn't look behind her, couldn't bear it, and then she was through and pressing the button on the other side so that it closed up tight.

Mij breathed.

Breathe: in and out.

She breathed until she could move again. To the living quarters, that tiny bubble on the top of the *Arrow*. To the only home, and the only people, she had left.

'I just want to go and take a look for myself,' said Lars.

Everything about him was ridiculous: his posture, his tone. That puffed-out chest. He was wearing only his boxer shorts, his hands on his hips. How soft and pale he looked, white-blond hair on his head, his arms, his chest, and delicate blue veins just under the surface of his skin. 'Don't be a fucking idiot,' she told him.

He lifted his chin and stared her down. 'Then what are you suggesting?'

'I don't know. Not that. I told you: there's something down there.'

Lars reached for his trousers, on the end of Salma's bed, and put them on. Salma, sitting up with the cover pulled over her chest, said, 'How certain are you of that?'

'One hundred per cent,' Mij told her. She couldn't afford to show any weakness over it. She glanced around Salma's bedroom. None of Lars' belongings, apart from his clothes, were visible. They weren't sharing the space, as yet. Why did that make a difference to her? She needed them both to be their own people. Not two against one in this. And being aggressive or unreasonable would only push them closer together, Mij realised. She took a deep breath, tried to calm herself, but it was so difficult. Everything had changed. 'Say, ninety-eight per cent. Tell me what else you think it could be.'

'You were scared. Stressed,' Salma said quietly, with precision. 'You've been anxious since the counter broke.'

'It's not that,' Mij told her.

'It isn't about casting doubt on you, but on your ability to perceive the situation accurately.'

'We need to see it,' Lars said, fully dressed now, his hands once more on his hips, in that heroic pose.

'I'm not going back down there, and neither should you,' said Mij. She was a coward, of course. All she wanted was to go home. Turn the ship around, return to Earth. There was no sustainable Earth to go back to, and no way to pilot the ship anyway. Everything was out of their hands. She had to go on. She swallowed, tried again. 'You won't find it. I can't even describe where it is. Everything's unmarked.'

Lars shrugged, as if that would make no difference to him. 'Just a quick look. Just to see.'

'Well, then,' said Salma. She threw back the cover and stood up, naked, then began to dress quickly. 'What? All this modesty, bravery, fear. All this. We'll go down there and you'll try to retrace your steps, as best as you can. One person can't say reality is whatever they've seen with their own eyes. Two people can only have an argument about it. You need three people to make a decision, okay?'

She was powerful, persuasive. Mij nodded. She watched Salma dress in her usual one-piece, pulling up the long zip to the hollow at the base of her throat.

'Let's go,' she said.

Later, over the facade of a lunchtime in which nobody ate, they talked it through.

At least the body had still been there, and she had found it. The shock on their faces had been considerable. She realised then that they had both thought she was having some kind of breakdown. But no, they were now united by what they had all seen. Salma was right. Three people together could make a decision.

What decision could they make?

Mij felt drenched in fear, permeated by it. It was changing her. She wasn't the person she once was, on this journey. But there could be strength in the three of them.

'I don't understand how there can be something down there,' said Lars. He coughed, pushed his food around his plate once more, then added, 'I mean, something that's been there the entire time. Surely there would be some sort of warning system on board. Or you would have seen – evidence – of it before, Mij, during your runs.'

'A warning system,' Mij said. 'For attacks on the canisters. For an animal, ripping it open.' The word *monster* came into her head, and she pushed it away quickly, firmly. That would be the last thing the situation needed. But once she had thought of it, she could not banish it from her own mind. What kind of animal could do a thing like that? The strength needed, the power, and then the precision of the dismembering. It was something else.

'If it really is an animal then we can go down there and catch it,' said Lars.

'You could try,' she retorted, then reminded herself: stop driving a wedge. It was so difficult to listen to his bullshit, but if Salma sided with him then she would be alone. If she kept slapping him down, she would only isolate herself.

'We have a responsibility to –'

'No, Mij is right,' said Salma. She was the only one managing to eat anything at all, and that was in meagre amounts: a few grains of rice from her fork, delicately lifted to her mouth, every now and then. 'Catch it with what? We have no weapons, no training. We cannot know what we're dealing with, except that its strong enough to rip open a sealed canister. Plus we are jumping to conclusions. Possibly the canister malfunctioned, split open from the inside –'

'The claw marks!' said Lars, incredulously, and Mij felt a brief twinge of solidarity with him.

'What it looks like is not the same as what it is. Besides, we were all on edge, all frightened, with only seconds to look at the situation. We're not scientists or soldiers. We're not trained to operate under pressurised conditions like that. We're caretakers until we arrive. Let's not forget that.' She took a tiny mouthful of rice.

It was the most Mij had ever heard her say. Was Salma in charge now? That was not a description that was meant to apply to any of them.

'We should at least try,' said Lars, in a tight, hard voice. His hands had formed fists. It reminded Mij of the hands of the body. Those curled fingers.

'There are so many people down there,' Salma said. 'So many. Whatever is happening, even if it is a wild animal, it cannot even begin to affect the numbers of those who will survive this journey. That's all we need to think about. We leave the door sealed from now on. We don't go down there until we arrive.'

Lars shook his head, slowly, then said, 'And when we arrive?'

'We make weapons, we make plans. We utilise the resources of the new planet. And then we'll be able to let it off this ship, rather than being trapped in here with it.'

Keep the door sealed. A problem to be solved later. 'Sounds good,' Mij said. She felt her heartbeat slowing, her mind calming. Nothing needed to be done.

Lars stood up, and left the kitchen, his back rigid, unforgiving. Salma watched him go, and then took another tiny mouthful of rice.

'Do you think he'll...'

'He's all mouth and no trousers,' said Salma. The expression was so unexpected, so tartly said, that Mij felt an astonishing surge of amusement, and began to laugh. Salma didn't join in. 'What?' she said. 'He can't help it, so let's not hold it against him.'

'Where did you even hear that? All mouth and no trousers.'

'I took my undergraduate degree in London.' She smiled – a smile of secrets, some shared, some kept. Another forkful of rice. Mij knew better than to ask her questions. But the conversation, the laughter, had left her able to eat. Not meat. Possibly never meat again, but rice, clean and tidy in its bowl; she picked up her fork, and dug in.

Life went on. For a large percentage of them.

Lars didn't make an appearance at the counter check (0679991, 0003000, 5858588) that evening, but he turned up for supper, and was the one to suggest it was time to move on the usual round of Numbers. It was an obvious attempt to find some normality, but a welcome one. Still, they hadn't played for long before Lars faked his yawn and Salma followed suit. Mij couldn't believe either of them were tired in the least.

They wanted time alone, of course. Time to discuss what had happened.

Mij thought it over, and refused to yawn in reply. If there was a conversation about their situation to be had, she wanted to be present.

'Not tired?' Lars asked her. He stood next to the screen, fingers tapping the wall. 'It's been a hell of a day.'

'Not yet,' she said.

'Another round, then?'

'Why not?'

Lars nodded, then said, 'All right. Let's do: amount with life functions ceased.'

From her seat at the table Salma said, 'No,' instantly, loudly, and Lars stared her down.

'That's not how the manifest works,' Mij said, but even though she was close to Lars, he did not seem to hear her. She was invisible for the sake of this conversation; it was a two-way battle.

'You're scared,' Lars said.

'The data is based on the information passengers supplied before boarding,' Salma replied. 'Date of birth, occupation, hobbies...'

'So, it won't hurt to type it in.'

'Listen, I'm not –'

'Just guess,' he said. 'Guess.'

Salma pursed her lips. She said, 'One.'

'One?'

'Just the one we saw.'

'This isn't just about whatever happened to that canister. What about – natural wastage?'

Salma said, 'Describe to me what you mean by the term *natural wastage.*' She pronounced the words with careful disdain. Mij suddenly wished she'd gone to bed when she had the chance.

'Some canisters might have malfunctioned, say. Some people couldn't be kept alive any more, for whatever reason. '

'What reason?'

'I don't know that! How could I possibly know that? I know nothing about how this works, and neither do you!'

'Ten,' said Mij. 'I guess ten.' Just to get him to stop shouting. Besides, the manifest would never accept the command. She felt certain of it. And then this conversation could be forgotten.

'I guess a thousand,' said Lars.

The number – just the mention of it – was shocking. She exchanged a glance with Salma. A warning was contained in Salma's eyes. A plea. For what? For the idea that the cargo was intact, apart from that rogue incident. It could not have been caused by anything more than a freak malfunction. Or one animal. One lone animal, desperate for food. Say it had been locked in there since the beginning, and it ate a person a week – how many people would that be? She couldn't recall how long they'd been travelling, but surely it would be up around... It could easily be...

PASSENGER MANIFEST
QUERY?

LIFE FUNCTIONS CEASED: 78,321

'That's not right,' said Salma. 'It can't be right. We should turn it off and stop playing this stupid. Fucking. Game.'

She walked out of the room.

Drive or Be Driven

Lars looked only at the screen. Mij wasn't even certain he'd noticed Salma's departure. 'That must be an error,' she said.

His silence said everything he might have voiced. How could they know? How could they ever know anything? They had no skills between them. Mij had been a clerk, working in the admin team, but she only knew how to input data, not how to deal with damaged systems. When she'd made the final cut and Doctor Troon had congratulated her in person, she had asked: *Why me?* And Troon had replied: *It had to be you, and you alone. I knew it as soon as you came here.*

But I've got no skills: Mij had said.

Just be yourself. You've got no attachments, no family left. You're self-sufficient. You can be true to yourself. That's the key.

She had taken the doctor's word for it. If only she had bothered to learn anything about Arrow. Anything. Even if it was only how to disconnect a screen.

'It's an error,' she repeated, then left the kitchen, left the long row of numbers behind, and ran down the corridor to the sleeping quarters. It lasted less than thirty seconds; how tiny the living area was, compared to that vast space below, with so many canisters, so many lives, being carried.

Could it be right?

She thought about knocking on Salma's door and decided against it.

In her own room, she showered. Looked hard at the soft single bed, imagined being propped upright in a hard metal container instead. Stored, like luggage. Vulnerable to whatever lay outside it.

Mij got into bed. There were no yawns in her to give, but still, somehow, she slept.

Lars had a hammer in his hand.

'What are you doing?' Mij said. The passenger manifest screen was still intact; he hadn't smashed it yet. He was poised, hammer raised.

'It's not working,' he said. He dropped his hand, stepped back from the screen.

'Leave it alone.' The thought of it being destroyed added to her fear. So many things were out of control. She'd woken suddenly, feeling certain something was wrong. Thank God she had entered the galley at that moment. Just a few seconds later, and it would have been too late to stop him.

'I thought maybe I could get into it, mend it –' Lars said.

'No, you didn't.'

His eyes flared wide, and for a moment she thought he would simply go ahead and smash it, to defy her: to teach her a lesson, even. But he dropped his gaze and moved to the table to run his hand across an open canvas roll of tools, laid out there. She had never seen it before. He slid the hammer back into an empty pocket and tied the roll shut.

'We can't just do nothing,' he said.

'Where did these come from?'

'They were my grandfather's.'

A sentimental attachment, then. But also a symbol. The illusion of control, as if things could be repaired. Mended. Mij saw it clearly in the way he touched the roll. But still the truth remained. If Lars couldn't mend it – and none of them could – then he would try to destroy it.

'Sit,' she said, trying to inject warmth into her voice. 'I'll make breakfast. Is Salma still asleep?'

'I don't know. I didn't – I stayed in my own room last night.'

'Okay.' She wanted to ask – *how long have you been together?* But that felt insensitive. He answered the unspoken question anyway.

'It's only been a couple of weeks.'

'That's good,' she said. She took the instant oats from the cupboard, divided it between bowls. In the wake of Lars' silence, she added, 'I only mean – it's not that I'm totally unobservant, then. I've only been suspicious about you both for a couple of weeks.'

'Suspicious?'

170

'That you were...'

'Ah, I understand.'

'It's so difficult,' she added, on an impulse, 'to make real connections any more. I don't mean sex, so much as being understood. We're all out of practice, with only each other for company.'

'We should try harder, maybe.'

'Yeah.' The microwave did its job, and she watched the seconds count down to zero. Then she took out the bowls and carried them to the table. One for her, one for Lars. Next to his roll of tools. The material was well-worn, and he left one hand upon it, resting. Protective. She grabbed spoons from the cupboard drawer, then took her seat and started to eat.

'We can't just do nothing,' Lars repeated.

Careful – thought Mij. It wasn't only a lack of practice at being understood, but the act of wanting to be understood. Of going that extra step to make connections. But she had to.

'You won't be running down in the cargo deck any more,' Lars said. He picked up the spoon, stirred the porridge.

'No, I won't.'

'But there's nowhere else you can run.'

He was right. The treadmill in the store room had broken right at the beginning of the voyage, only moving jerkily backwards when it was turned on. But there was still the rowing machine, and the weights. A small utility room at the back of the store held all kinds of exercise equipment; she decided to have a look through it, later. 'Maybe you could mend the treadmill,' she said. 'With your tools.'

'I'm not much of a – yes, I'll try, though. Okay. Look. I didn't mean to keep them a secret, but I just – it's just to remember him by. My grandfather.'

'It's fine. But please don't – don't use them on the screen, okay? Nothing related to the ship. We should all talk about it before we attempt anything like that.'

'My wife is down there,' he said. He put down his spoon. 'My wife is in the cargo deck.'

'We don't have attachments,' Mij said. 'No links to the passengers. I was told that was one of the reasons why I got this job.'

'I lied. Saw this all coming, years ago, so my wife and I – we lived separately. She's American, you see. A security risk, rival projects. Arrow wouldn't even have considered her. I bribed –'

'No, no,' Mij said.

'I'm not – I realise –'

'Does Salma know?'

He bowed his head. 'No.'

'Fucking hell. Fucking hell.'

'So we have to do something.'

'We can't –'

'We're smart people. Let's come up with a plan. We can try to save as many as possible.'

'Is she – still alive?'

'I have no idea. The manifest will let me search for certain things. Her hometown, her likes. But there's always more than one person in each category. Sometimes hundreds. Sometimes thousands.'

'But never zero,' Mij said.

He blinked. 'I need your help,' he said.

'You need to tell Salma.'

Lars shook his head.

'What happens when we get there? Mij asked him. 'Your wife gets defrosted and you all make up a happy threesome?'

'Don't be ridiculous. She's probably already dead, if those numbers on the screen were correct, right? And we'll probably never get there. The counter is out of control, the screen shows crazy figures. The entire ship is probably taking us nowhere. We're all fucking doomed, Mij. Let me try to save my wife.'

'While still fucking your girlfriend.'

'Girlfriend,' he repeated. He mulled the word over, then said, 'I don't think it's that serious.'

She couldn't help it. Laughter clawed its way up, through her throat, and she couldn't stop.

'What's so funny?' said Salma, from the doorway.

A stupid plan.

A plan with 0.0001 per cent chance of working. Less than that.

Mij held the badminton net in front of her, bunched in her hands. Behind her, Salma carried part of the pole from the basketball goal. Lars had the hammer. A few paces in front, he crouched low and moved like a crab, sidling forward, along the walkway. He had the hammer permanently raised above his head. He looked ridiculous. They all did.

They continued down the walkway.

What if it's enormous? Salma had asked them both, after they'd run through their decision to attempt to catch it. *What if this stuff won't do the job?*

Then we run: said Lars. *But at least we will have tried.*

Mij added: *I think we need to try.*

The numbers had switched. Two against one, now on the side of action. Salma didn't need to be told that. She'd simply agreed, and they'd made their weapons.

Mij didn't really understand why she had swapped sides. It wasn't only to do with Lars, and his plea. It was something to do with the fear she felt. Could the animal – monster, even – be worse than that fear? She had to find out.

'How many markers have you used?' whispered Salma, from behind her.

'Seven,' said Mij.

'Have you got enough left? Be sure you don't run out.' It was a simple idea: whenever they had made a turn from the first walkway, Mij had dropped a bent nail from a pouch she carried, made by tying one of her jogging tops around her waist. That way they could retrace their steps when they turned around, but using markers that were unobtrusive enough so that they could not be spotted by something that might track them.

That was a disturbing thought. Being tracked. But why would an animal track them unless it was intelligent enough to work out their plan, and counter it with a hunt of its own?

Onwards.

They were ridiculous, yes, like a children's book Mij had liked, as a little girl, going hunting through the woods, over a river, moving in single file with eyes trained on the surroundings: *Where is it? Where is it?* The children had been armed with buckets, spades, nets, sticks. A game, played. She had read it over and over, fascinated by their togetherness, as an only child. She didn't understand what togetherness meant. Her parents didn't care for games, for hunts and finding. Her mother had been prickly, standoffish, and her father argumentative. Where had she fitted within their family? As soon as she was old enough to attend boarding school they had gone off again, travelling, just as they had done before she was created. She had always felt like an intrusion into their lives.

'Have you got enough?' Salma whispered again, her voice panicked, testy.

'It's fine,' Mij told her.

They moved onwards.

It was the absolute facelessness of the storage deck, without signs, without deviation. To get lost down here... It was impossible to remember the sense of peace she had once found here, in this vast space, running. She had concentrated only on her strides, her breathing, in a cavern filled with frozen thousands, their eyes closed, their brains and hearts slowed to a stop. Sealed so tightly in canisters. It had seemed so safe, but now – all of these people were helpless, vertically buried. If they woke there could be no help. Only the smooth silver surface of the canister an inch from your screaming face.

What was it easier to dream about, to find in your nightmares: the depths of space and the silver canisters, or the slow starvation of an exhausted Earth?

She was suddenly grateful that her parents were both dead. They had never been able to ask her to smuggle them onboard, or say a stilted goodbye.

Lars stopped.

'Three thousand,' he said.

Where were they? He had told them he had a plan – counting canisters, making a certain number of turns to cover the most ground effectively. If they had walked past three thousand frozen people, it had not seemed like it to Mij. Still, she trusted his counting.

'Marker here,' he said. His body was angled to the right, his attention on the next walkway.

Mij took out a nail and bent it to a right angle. She placed it so the point indicated where they would go next, at the crossroads. Lars stepped over it and she did the same, following, listening to Salma's footsteps behind. Yes, there she was, and the sharpened tip of the pole swung into Mij's peripheral vision for a moment.

Onwards.

Mij pictured an animal.

Claws, long ones. Strength. Bunched muscles in the shoulders. Fur? She thought of a documentary she had seen about bears, using restored footage from a time when they had even roamed free, in places. It could be a bear. No, that was only on her mind because of the book she had loved in her childhood, surely. All bears were extinct, and her mind was bringing just another level of stupidity to this situation. There was no way a bear could be on board. A thought came to her: *perhaps not everything stowed away in the canisters is human.* The owners of the *Arrow* might have put other species into storage, planning to populate the new planet with more than humanity. A Noah's Ark experiment. Two by two. And a malfunction had woken one, and it had clawed its way out, and then got hungry... Finally, something that almost made

175

sense. She could tell the others, get it straight in her head, explain it –

She collided with the wall of Lars' back. The net, stretched between her hands, tangled in the pouch of nails. Carefully, she separated them, so the nails didn't spill out, her attention focused on the task. Salma said, 'What?' in a voice so small, so uncomprehending, and Lars said, 'Look. Look.' Something in his tone made her certain that she didn't want to see whatever had stopped him in his tracks.

Mij looked.

The first part of the walkway was normal. A hundred untouched canisters, maybe more. Then all destroyed. Every single one, both sides, as far down as she could see. The bodies forming mounds. Not torn apart, like the one she had found. These ones still had their heads. The blank expressions of the frozen. So many of them. Far too many to count.

A massacre.

A touch on her shoulder: she flinched, realised Salma was right behind her, sagging. She took her weight.

Lars, ahead of them both, took a step forward.

'No,' said Salma. 'Lars.'

He kept moving forwards, in that crablike crouch, until he reached the first of the bodies. He stopped to look it over; Mij was glad she could only see his back. She wouldn't have wanted to see his expression as he stared into that face. He moved to the next body, then the next, picking up pace, overturning them in their stiff, grasping postures, running his hands over them.

He was looking for his wife.

Mij couldn't move, could only watch his hunt.

The feeling of being watched: it returned, so strong. Just like last time. Like finding the first body.

'We need to go,' said Salma. 'Lars. Lars!'

'Stop it,' Mij whispered. Salma's voice was so loud. Lars was working fast now, clumsily, pushing at bodies where they had heaped, clambering over them.

Ahead of him, perhaps fifty paces away, she saw a movement. Someone was alive, pulling themselves out from a pile of corpses. Mij's chest tightened: she couldn't breathe, couldn't speak. The hope of it. She knew the moment Salma saw it too, by the grip on her shoulder, painfully tight.

Lars kept searching. Why wouldn't he look up, look ahead? Mij finally found the ability to move, taking steps towards the carnage, leading Salma, as the survivor shook themselves free, climbed to stand erect, naked, slick with blood. Shining under the bright lights of the deck – the skin was strange, almost liquid. And the face was featureless. No eyes, no nose: only a puckered hole where a mouth should be. Not a survivor. Something else.

A piercing sound, so raw. Salma, screaming.

The noise snapped Lars from his search, pulled his head upright. He saw the shape and stood up, and their stances mirrored each other. A challenge. He raised his hammer, that familiar pose, arm pulled back.

'No,' Mij said, her throat rough, hoarse. She lifted the net, like a shield. Behind her, Salma was moaning, a deep, wrenched word that could have been: *run*.

The hole in the centre of the shape's face began to expand. It pulled back to reveal blank space within: not black, not white, not any colour, but there was the suggestion of something inside, pressing to get out. It bulged, spewed forth and coagulated to create itself again – another shape, red and slick and tall. Two of them.

A loud clatter on her left; Mij jumped back. It was the basketball pole hitting the walkway. Salma's grip was gone from her shoulder; she risked a look behind her and saw that Salma was running fast, running away. Every instinct told her to do the same – but Lars, Lars was squaring up, moving forward. She couldn't leave him. She dropped down, felt for the pole, and grasped it, straightened up with the net in one hand and the pole in the other.

The first shape retracted. No longer human, the arms and legs subsumed into the torso, and everything sucked upwards into the hole in the face, turning itself inside out, hanging in mid-air. It hurt to look at that colourless space inside, like a membrane stretched over terrible things, awful things. The new shape moved forward, long strides, and reached for Lars, who raised his hammer, brought it down fast upon the crown of its head. The head split apart with the blow, peeled into two long, thin liquid spikes that swiped forward and stuck into Lars' neck, then lifted his head free from his body, and turned it over and over with agility before bringing the head to the puckered hole which expanded so it could be swallowed.

Lars' body fell. The hammer clattered to the walkway.

Mij threw the pole. She threw it with a speed and accuracy she did not know she was capable of, and it stuck firm in the chest of the new shape for a moment before it reached for the pole and pulled it free, letting it fall next to Lars' hammer.

The process began again. The central hole expanded further until it ate its own body, sucking in the limbs and torso. Then it vomited out a long stream of red liquid that formed a fresh human shape, which reached for the next body it could find.

They were multiplying.

Mij dropped the net and ran.

She nearly missed the marker of the first nail. By sheer luck she looked down and spotted it, and made the turn. Then she focused only on the nails, following the next, then the next, her breath getting shorter, heavier, but beyond everything there was the calm, clear voice in her head, telling her she had the speed and strength she needed. She had her legs, her arms, her head. She would keep them.

Another turn, another, another, and there was the door, in the distance. No sign of Salma: would she have gone through, not waited for them? Mij accelerated, sprinted full-out, using her reserves. Reached the door, pressed the button, fell through the open doorway, and found she was alone.

Salma.

She couldn't leave without her. Lars was gone, dead without a doubt. Not Salma. Mij had to be sure she was safe. But it was so hard to turn around, to look back at the deck.

The first walkway was empty. The canisters, silver and smooth, were in their rows.

She dragged herself to the door and dared to call out.

'Salma!'

The word reverberated around the hold. Echoed, amplified.

Please don't be dead.

No. No, Salma must have run all the way back upstairs, to the living quarters. Mij could picture her in her bed, under it, shivering, hiding. It was understandable. Salma could be a coward just as long as she wasn't dead.

There was a sound from deep in the deck.

Was it an echo?

'Mij!'

A voice. Salma's voice, but from so far away and from everywhere, too, echoed and amplified and lost in its own reflections.

'This way!' Mij called. Her words echoed everywhere.

A reply: garbled, reverberating.

Like a dream, like a slow dream, a shape came into view. One of them. It walked forward, along the walkway, not fast. In an even stride. As she stood there, the central hole of its featureless face came into view clearly. The liquid skin was running in rivulets down its body, puckering as the hole expanded.

Mij stepped back and punched the button. The door closed.

She waited.

For a sound, for something. For Salma's bang on the door. For the shape to break through. Could it? If it could rip open canisters, why not the door? Nothing made sense. She waited for Lars to appear, to wake her up.

How many walkways were there? How many ways to turn? She could imagine Salma missing a nail, running onwards in panic, then realising her mistake and taking random turns, getting deeper and deeper into the maze.

Now there was no hope. There was only the shut door.

She couldn't leave, couldn't bear to walk away, knowing Salma was in there. Lars, too. Even though she had watched him die, it was so difficult to leave him. It felt like a betrayal. His bravery. His fucking idiocy.

'We could have left it closed,' she said to the door. 'We could have left you closed.' It was soothing to say. She repeated it, over and over, and then the sounds mutated into humming, and she shifted her weight from one leg to the other, like a dance. Counting each step. One two three four. Upwards. By the time she got to a thousand and nothing had killed her, she had nothing left but the desire to sleep, to find a better dream than this.

She climbed the ladder to the living quarters.

It was a monster. They were monsters, more of them, getting strong, growing in numbers. She checked Salma's room first. It was empty, of course. Lars' room, too. The galley, empty, with the words

PASSENGER MANIFEST
QUERY?

strong on the screen.

Then to the gym. Then the observation deck, to the window, with the fixed stars behind her. The counter was clicking over.

9.544867
0.0576224
183.333333

Mij slumped beside it, and watched it turn.

The daily routine slipped away from her so fast.

After waking on the observation deck to find herself still alive, still alone, she retreated to her room and let time pass. All sense of day and night left her. What meal had they eaten before going down to the cargo deck? Breakfast, lunch. Supper. They hadn't played Numbers, and that was a supper thing. She couldn't remember the last time they had all played Numbers.

At first, every time she woke, she thought Salma was back. What would be the probability of that: to randomly find a way out of the vast desk, avoid however many monsters were living, breeding, down there, and return upstairs to her own bed? She saw Salma's face everywhere for a while, and then she saw it in a dream, melting, wiped free of features, and that puckered hole growing, spreading, to take up everything and swallow it down.

Why did these things not break down the door? Why could they not, with their arms and legs, simply press the button and open the door for themselves? But she was powerless if any of these eventualities came to pass, so she simply stopped worrying about it. Better to be asleep when they came. Better not to know.

Mij woke thirsty, starving, desperate to pee.

The body could not be denied. It had its own clock; not a time of day or night so much as a certainty of what had to be done to keep moving forwards.

She dragged herself out of bed and used the toilet, then drank from the tap, handfuls of clean running water. To the kitchen. She took the first packet from the cupboard and heated it through. Rice. The memory of eating rice with Lars and Salma came to her, so strongly, triggered by the smell, the texture in her mouth. Lars' wrap of tools, missing the nails and hammer, still lay on the table; she ate tentatively, trying not to look at it.

She felt the urge to return to the storage deck and call out Salma's name.

It would do no good, objectively. There was no way for Salma to follow the sound, even if she were still alive. And she couldn't possibly be alive. How many people could still be alive, down there? There were so many passengers, but that only meant so many bodies for the monsters to take, to use.

She finished the rice and crossed to the screen.

PASSENGER MANIFEST

QUERY?

Lars had asked a question that had sparked this need to find answers, to hunt out whatever lived in the cargo deck. She typed it in again:

LIFE FUNCTIONS CEASED:

242,017

Such a long number.

It blinked out, the screen returning to black. Then a new number took its place:

265,574

It had never done this before. The new number winked out, and was replaced with another:

329,987

446,644

531,122

'Stop that,' she told the screen.

594,466

'Stop. Stop. Stop.'

626,698

751,100

Mij slammed her hand against the screen. She wanted to reach in and rip the numbers out, anything to stop them increasing.

885,573

The shapes. One had become two, four, sixteen. The shapes, ripping open the canisters and making more of themselves, over and over.

922,741

Travelling, to reach a distant destination. If they reached it, who would be left alive?

1,005,878

It couldn't keep getting higher, it couldn't, real or not, nightmare or malfunction or monster. Mij staggered to the table, flipped open the roll of tools, pulled out one by its smooth wooden handle. It was a chisel. It had a reality, in her hand, that the numbers could never match.

She took it over to the wall.

1,258,600

Thinking of Lars and his hammer – of how she had stopped him completing this very action – she raised the chisel and brought the point of it down on the bottom left corner of the screen. It dug in, made a small crack in the glass. She aimed for the same spot again, and this time the screen splintered, the crack widening across the length of the glass.

The number winked out and was not replaced.

Mij felt a weight lift from her chest. She breathed slowly, deeply. It was not that anything had been achieved by the destructive action, no monster defeated here, but to be free of the passenger manifest was a victory in itself. The numbers had carried such weight.

The cracked screen toppled forwards, out of the wall. It landed on the black and white tiles, the crash loud, shocking.

Behind it, there were no wires. Nothing had held it in place, and the force of the chisel must have dislodged it; the screen had simply been jammed into the wall. And the wall was not solid at all. She stepped over the flat, plain back of the screen and looked into the gap. Wooden joists, plasterboard. A cavity. No cables, no pipes. No electricity.

The screen could never have worked.

But it had. It had. They had all seen it, played Numbers many times, typed in so many queries. Mij put the chisel to the edge of the keyboard, below the hole, and applied force, hitting the handle with the heel of her hand. The keyboard popped free at one corner. She wrenched it from the wall easily. It was flimsy in design, and a panel down one side allowed access; she used the chisel again and the keyboard split in half. There was nothing inside. Both halves were only moulded plastic.

The cavity left in the wall was the same as the first. Wood, plaster. Like a set, for a film. An attempt at reality designed to fool those who did not look too hard.

Mij returned to the microwave, fiddled with the dial. The number of seconds and minutes on the display grew and shrank as she turned it one way, then the other. Was that real? It had to be – the food always came out hot. She couldn't risk breaking it, so she carefully made a hole in the wall behind it, digging with the chisel, and peered inside. No wires, no pipes.

On some level, in its nuts and bolts and electrics and mechanics, this was not a real ship.

The observation deck.

She ran there, skidded to a halt in front of that unchanging view of space. It was static, predictable. Had the dots of light ever changed position, looked different? She couldn't remember it.

She turned to the counter – the measure of space travelled. Its malfunction had signalled the beginning of doubt for them all. Such random numbers, each bearing no relation to the last.

0000000

'Click over,' she said.

0000000

'Click over, click over.'

0000000

She was caught unawares by the crash.

The sudden, grinding halt of the *Arrow* flung across the deck, and she hit the window with her shoulder, the pain radiating upwards to her neck, immediate and intense. She got her breath back and managed to stand, rubbed the shoulder. It didn't seem seriously hurt. She had been lucky; she could have broken something, or hit her head. Things were confusing enough without a concussion.

The view from the window was different.

No stars. No black.

The view was a soft, dark blue.

Her heart contracted in her chest: *a sky. Possibly atmosphere. Gravity?* Perhaps the counter had not been lying, this time, after all, and the *Arrow* had hit its target.

What came next?

184

Mij looked around for the chisel, spotted it across the deck, by the door. She scrambled to it and held it close. There were instructions she had been given for this moment. All three of them had memorised them. She couldn't recall them. Canisters warming, opening; passengers waking; the door to the cargo deck and the main hatch to the outside world opening: she couldn't have done these things even if she remembered how.

The dark blue sky was slowly changing colour. She watched it deepen further to purple, then fade to black.

That was when she realised: she couldn't let them out.

The window of the observation deck revealed a pattern of day and night. The days had light skies, and wisps of clouds. There was nothing else visible in the view, so she saw nothing of the ground upon which the *Arrow* rested, she imagined. She would have loved to see land. Trees, maybe. In her mind, it was Earth. An untouched, pristine Earth. Although she had felt the lurch and bang of the *Arrow*'s landing, she imagined it had touched down so softly, hardly stirring a long stretch of wild green grass.

Mij couldn't let the monsters have it.

After the landing she had checked that the exit hatch remained securely shut, climbing the ladder, and putting her hands to the metal. It was locked up tight. On the way back down the ladder she slipped, nearly lost her footing, and had clung to the rungs, waiting for the panic to subside. The idea of falling, of hurting herself, was both terrifying and laughable.

During the daylight hours she took the chisel to the observation window. It was nothing like the screen of the passenger manifest. Thick and tough, it took her days to even make a small white scar on it, in the lower corner where she could sit as she worked. She aimed for the same spot over and over again, ignoring the pain in her hands. When blisters formed on her palms she wrapped them in her old jogging clothes and carried on.

When night fell on new Earth Mij took herself off to the kitchen and ate, keeping her eyes averted from the holes in the walls, the screen, and the keyboard. It was no good to doubt everything, for some things were real whether she believed in them or not. Better to commit to the act of trying than to simply doubt, and lie still.

But sometimes her body demanded stillness. Sleep remained a refuge when it was dark outside the window. Mij would put herself to bed, as she had done, as she would continue to do, until something changed. Until there was an end.

She woke to the sound of singing.

Mij sat up.

It was a woman's voice. The song was one she knew – an old favourite of hers from Earth, about stormy weather and umbrellas. It brought sudden, uncontrollable emotion, and she realised she was crying. She scrambled out of bed, didn't bother to dress. She followed the voice to Salma's bedroom.

Salma. She was back. She had made it out of the labyrinth.

By the time the door slid open Mij had convinced herself that she would see that familiar face; it took far too long to realise she was looking at a different woman, standing tall in a black suit, with her hair pinned up and her hands clasped behind her back. She stopped singing and looked Mij up and down without any surprise.

It was Doctor Troon.

She was frowning, of course. Mij remembered that as her natural expression; everything was serious when it came to the journey. At the end of one briefing Doctor Troon had seen Mij smiling – she couldn't remember why – and had snapped, 'Smile when you get there.' Where had Lars and Salma been during that briefing? She couldn't remember that, either.

Troon said, 'You promised me you would concentrate. I explained the dangers of not concentrating.'

'How are you here?' Mij asked her. 'Have you always been here?'

'I made you memorise your instructions. You know the answer to this.'

Mij walked forward slowly, reached out, and touched the doctor's sleeve. The material was stiff, quite cool. Troon was not a projection or a recording; she was there. She was real.

'Oh God,' Mij said. The sheer relief of being in the presence of another person was overwhelming. She was not alone. She stepped forward to put her arms around the doctor, who shrugged her off and moved to the bed, putting distance between them.

'I'm here for this,' she said.

She picked up the framed photograph that Salma kept on her bedside table and looked at it long and hard.

'Everyone else is dead,' Mij said. It was so hard to get the words out.

'Of course, they are. You knew this would happen. You told me you could cope with it.'

'I didn't – I never thought – they were all killed, everyone was killed –'

'That's one way to look at it.'

'You have to help me. I can't leave. I can't let them out.'

For the first time she saw Troon's expression soften. 'But you have to.'

'They're monsters!'

'Remember the procedures. We went over it and over it. This was always going to be difficult, but you're so close now. You've arrived.' She came back to Mij's side, patted her shoulder awkwardly, then handed her the photograph. 'Look,' she said. 'Look.'

Mij stared at the image: the mother, the father, the baby. In the background, the bright colours of canvas market stalls, goods on sale. She wondered if the photograph had been taken in Egypt, where Salma was born. Egypt: another place, another press of people that no longer existed. Perhaps that's why Salma had never mentioned her past – it was simply too painful to recall every loss.

How very like her mother Salma had been, judging by the photo. Small and slim, and intent in expression. It was a surprising resemblance, like finding Salma, fresh, in the long ago. Standing beside her father, but her father was Lars.

She checked the face carefully. It was definitely Lars. Tall, blond, at an unflattering angle with his face slightly turned away, but it was him. In her hands was a photograph of Salma and Lars. Once Mij had seen the truth of it, it couldn't be unseen. And the baby. And the baby –

'The baby is me,' she said to Doctor Troon. 'Me with my family. Salma is my mother and Lars is my father.' She realised it, understood it. The knowledge was in her bones.

'This is your reality,' said Troon. 'Concentrate.'

The word was powerful, attached to a memory that could no longer remain hidden.

Concentrate. There's only room for one: Doctor Troon had said. *Everything rests on you.*

Only room for one? The *Arrow* was huge, wasn't it?

I don't know what will happen. I suspect you'll try to construct a reality that makes sense of the journey. The danger is that you'll lose yourself in that reality, and forget what needs to be done.

A snatch of the past was not enough. Mij closed her eyes, attempted to recall it all. It simply wouldn't come to her. In the darkness behind her eyelids she felt pressure, containment, as if she were trapped in a tiny, cold space.

When she opened her eyes Doctor Troon was gone.

So was Salma's room.

She was standing by the door of the cargo hold.

The photograph was still in her hands. A baby, a mother, and a father at a market, like so many markets all over the world. She had been so young – too young to remember that moment. A moment in which a couple celebrated, showed off their act of multiplication to be captured by the camera.

She looked around, saw that the ladder back to the upper deck was gone and the hatch sealed up. There was no escape. But the door remained the same. Wait – there was one difference. Below the button that operated the opening mechanism a counter had appeared, just like the one on the observation deck. It was clicking over, clicking down, at a steady pace.

0000993

0000992

0000991

It had all been an illusion. The illusion of time and space passing, of talking and playing games and reading, of monsters and murder. Lars and Salma had been reconstructions of her own parents: argumentative and difficult, quiet, and withdrawn. They had kept her company throughout, making her feel excluded once more, as they always had.

No, nothing had been real apart from the journey itself. If there was nothing else to hold on to, at least there was that fact. She would keep it in her vision, just like the boy in the novel by her bedside who had stared so hard at his toes.

Concentrate.

The counter continued to click down, backwards.

0000954

0000953

0000952

Mij sat down, slipped off her shoes, pulled off her socks. She stared at her toes. They looked the same to her as they had always done. The skin smooth, the nails short. And yet she couldn't remember cutting them, even once, while on board the *Arrow*.

Then it came to her.

This was not a journey forwards, through space. It was a journey backwards, through time.

She remembered. She remembered it all.

'Concentrate,' says Doctor Troon. 'Hold the answer in your head, for when you arrive in the past. We have no idea how the human mind will interpret time travel. You may experience confusion, anxiety, depression, hallucinations. Nothing matters but completing the task.'

'The task,' Mij repeats. It is a long list of actions and knowledge, to be undertaken upon arrival in the past. A carefully worked out plan to get the leaders to listen to her, take her seriously. She has memorised it, but right now not one single step will come to mind. All that she can think is this: *I have to save the world.*

How melodramatic it sounds. Mij, the chosen one, on a quest to save humanity, like in the pages of a fantasy novel. She only half-believes it herself – the possibility of time travel. Ridiculous. But she'll get in the canister, for the sake of the idea that things can be changed, and the Earth can find a future different from this one. No more war, no more hunger. No choking fumes and spreading diseases, dirty water, dying trees. A sustainable solution. That's as far-fetched as a time machine.

But here she stands, with her photograph of herself and her parents, all together, clutched to her chest. A memento of a time when they all looked happy, even though she couldn't quite believe they ever had been. So why not believe in a fantasy?

'I'm ready,' she says.

She moves backwards, one slow step at a time, manoeuvring until she is inside the upright canister. It is silver and cigar-shaped, only big enough for one person. It is only a tiny part of the machine itself, of course; a moving part that will be accelerated to an astonishing speed within a track, built around some other, much bigger moving part that is covered from view and which Mij has never seen. So much of all this remains a mystery, apart from the cost. Arrow Industries lies on the verge of bankruptcy, the media reports. Our last, best hope that has sucked up all the remaining resources. She doesn't understand the science, and she's afraid of it.

Doctor Troon nods, and closes the door.

She didn't even say *goodbye*, or *good luck*. The canister is close around her. For a moment Mij holds her breath, then forces herself to breathe normally.

She waits. She waits to save the world.

But – it comes to her now, only now, just as everything will change – that she will also destroy the world. She will travel back in time, and her presence will alter the course of everyone's lives. There are thoughts that will not be had, experiences that will be lost. Different babies will be born and different people will die. It is mass murder, in a way. She can only hope that it works out better, but even if it does, even if it creates the best version of Earth that there can ever be – so many people will never take a breath because of her.

Time is a monster. A devouring monster that eats everyone up, and spits them out, over and over again. A monster that multiplies: seconds to minutes to hours to years, a never-ending countdown, and it has her head in its mouth.

'Let me out,' she says.

There's not enough room to lift her hands, bang her fists. She drums her feet, kicks them hard, on the metal. Feels pain through her toes. 'Let me out,' she shouts, 'Let me out let me out let me –'

Mij stares at her toes.

She can still feel the pain in them, as if it happened only a moment ago.

0000078

So much time has passed.

The walls of the room have closed in further. There's barely enough space to stand, but she manages it. She decides against putting on her shoes and socks. The counter is clicking over fast.

0000035

She watches it on its journey.

0000014

Behind the door there lurks monsters. If she presses the button, they will really exist. They will have killed everyone, remade everyone. Into what?

0000007

If only she could see into the cargo deck. She wants to believe that new, happy people wait beyond, ready to populate a clean and better Earth.

0000004

One. That's all there is. There is only one person, on a journey. Her instructions upon arrival are lost; perhaps she will remember them, if she presses the button. Perhaps not. Her mouth is dry. Her toes are sore. The walls are so close around her that she can't lift her hands.

0000001

The button is in front of her face. She cranes her neck forward and touches it with her forehead. It's warm and soft, like the hand of an older, wiser person. Everything will be all right. It always is, eventually.

0000000

The door swings back, and the light floods in.

Rich Growth

Let this growth be real and true. Let it be the start of a stalk that reaches the roof of the dome and spreads its seeds across the high jewelled panels. Let those seeds use my body to climb, to meet those jewels. Then let them bond, and bind, and create delicate flowers of many curves and lines and colours that I can sell for good solid profit, please. This is my fervent hope. I wish it every time I sink my feet into the soil and coax up the roots that wait there.

It's my patch, has been for years, and I know it well. It has a lot of life still to give, even though it's old, much older than Marty who taught me the ways of it. Marty died long ago, when I was barely trained, but today she's on my mind as I work. She was a friend of my mother's, and she decided she wanted me right from the start, at my birth. As soon as I came forth she said to my mother: *I'll take her.* She did wait until I was weaned before the trade was made, so I have a fleeting memory of my mother. Nothing more than a smile.

I've never thought anything bad of Marty's decision to make me hers from the beginning. I loved her lessons as soon as we began – and that was shortly after I could stand up tall and sturdy.

'Nearly time for market,' says Gretel, from the patch next to mine. She wipes her hands on her trousers and steps around the seedlings, making for the entryway. She's always early to leave and late to return; that's why her plants rarely make the dome. *Time is inches*, Marty used to say.

The feet go in the soil and the arms reach high. A good seedling uses the feet, then the legs, then takes itself off to the sky

193

once it can support itself, but a bad one will not detach from their human trellis, and if a gardener does not spot it early it'll slide inside the holes of the body, greedy seedling, and then anchor in the intestines. Then upwards, through the organs, the lungs. Marty told me she saw that happen four times, in her lifetime, and those growers had to be left in their patches, could not be pulled free. The seedlings became too strong in their grip inside the body, so there was nothing to be done but to feed and water the living frames until the tendrils erupted from their mouths and broke down their brains for food, putting an end to their suffering. Then the plants would die back, grown too fast and strong to survive without that cheap and easy supply of nutrients. A terrible waste of both plant and human.

I've not seen that myself, a fact of which I am glad. But then, there haven't been many growers in this dome for a long time, so less opportunity to see the worst things Marty spoke of. The patches themselves remain fertile, vivid in colour and promise, but who wants to give their child to a grower any more? People out there have fewer babies and live happier lives. The dome sees to that. It is good luck and good health, and I am lucky to be within it. At least, that is what the people who I trade with tell me. *Life gets better and better*, said one man. *The gemflowers see to that. Just touching them brings prosperity.*

And yet I have touched many and never felt rich. And they do not want to give their babies up any more, no matter how wonderful the gemflowers are.

Life out there is not real, Marty once said to me, although she didn't care to talk about it often. It might have been all she ever said on the subject; it's certainly all I remember, but then, I was very young when she said it. *Finally, old enough to listen properly, and understand. Stay close to the ground. Life out there is not real, and nobody needs anything they can't touch. It's all hopes and happiness. Slippery dreams.*

As if those things are bad! I have my own hopes, and I'm not immune to the idea of happiness. But she's right. From what I see of the market, so much sold there is not real. A potion to make you pretty, a ticket for a prize. They don't understand the gemflowers, but then, I don't either. They are the end of a process I facilitate. I prefer the words I recite and the plants that rise.

That should be all, in my life, I think. That should be enough for anyone.

But now, as I age and see the beginning of personal withering, I find I want to know that this patch will be tended once I lie down and die. So I've saved enough for a child of my own. Thirty gemflowers. There must surely be somebody out there who will exchange their own treasure for such a fortune. A child is solid and real. I can hold a child and train it and ensure the future remains like the past: grounded, here, between the dome and the dirt.

His mother is here again. I watch them, from a small distance.

When she comes to visit he is all smiles for her and full of chatter about the way things grow from small beginnings. These are the stories I tell him, every night. And his mother then departs with her fears assuaged, I suppose. She looks around the dome with such awe and trepidation. I've seen her stare up and then flinch, as if gemflowers might fall on her head and crack her skull. I would like to tell her how they descend on vines when they are ready, but we have not reached that time yet and, besides, Benny should show her, once he has made something to show. I think he will be happier once that has happened, and he might start to smile – a true smile – for me.

How does one so young learn to lie so well, and not even for his own gain? He fakes his happiness so that she is content with that hard choice she made in the market months ago. I have never enquired after her reason for selling; that is not my business. But I saw the relief in her eyes, the taste of salvation on her wet lips when she took my gemflowers. And the cost she knew she would pay when she hugged the boy goodbye.

We've reached the end of this visit. She hugs him one more time. He gives her that smile. Yes, it is meant to make her feel better, but I'm beginning to think it might also be part of the cost.

She has gone back to the world outside, the mother who no longer has a child. Benny stands in the small part of the patch I have set aside for his learning. He reaches up with his hands, and I feel him push down with his toes. It's good. I feel it begin to work. Pain can be a force for great good in the work of a grower.

No. He blocks it, wills himself to be strong, to concentrate on the task in hand, and the roots lose interest. They want nothing less than his fear and doubt. I can't tell him this – who would understand, at that age? I'm sure I didn't. And perhaps these things aren't exactly as I learned them from Marty. The knowledge has mutated as it has gestated in me. Marty thought plants prefer to grow to a steady head, but I've come to understand they are eager for emotion.

So I watch Benny practice for a while, and then I stand on my own soil and show him how it's done, willing my pride in the task to him. I feel him striving to understand. He's a good learner. One day he'll smile truly for me. It's not necessary, but it will help me forget the way the smile drops from his face once his mother's back has turned, and her figure is retreating.

At the top of the dome the jewels wait for my tendrils to reach them, but the strength it takes nowadays is exhausting. I tire more easily, but I have found such artistry to compensate. It only pains me that the two could not come together – then I would have rivalled the great growers of old: the ones Marty used to turn lyrical on. But it's not to be, and I know this is the beginning of loss.

The extra twists and turns I coax into the tendrils, though, are so wonderful to see. I urge them to be wise in their paths, to support each other, and some even listen. Those ones make it to the jewels. Then the seeds slip inside and the flowers bloom, and the vines erupt in a wonderful moment of fast, free, speedy life, like nothing seen in any other stage of growth. And the vines, so obedient, so willing to come, so docile in their desire to place the gemflowers into my hand!

Let this never end. Let this not be the last of the flowers I receive. See, my hopes are changing still.

Benny nods in agreement as the vine gives up its flower. It's blue, with depths of light and dark within its delicacy. I hold it out so he can see it clearly. He's watched me do this often. He is getting to be tall and strong – not muscled, but strong in the joints and the way he moves his head and holds my eyes when he talks, which isn't too often.

I pocket the gemflower, and say, 'Your turn.'

He steps on his patch and touches the stalk he's been coaxing for months. It's nearly there. A straight growth, direct, supporting itself with little green buttresses that grow back down into the ground. These are fast becoming Benny's trademark; Gretel and the others have commented on the elegant simplicity of them. He's so young. A rarity in this place.

The first time he reached the roof of the dome his mother was there, invited in, wanted. She understood he had skill, I think. But it did not bring her pride, as I had hoped. He was too deep in his pain to hide it from her, and when the gemflower came down he cried, cried as the little boy never had, and he said to his mother: *don't leave me, don't leave me.* He put his thin arms around her and tried to keep her, but she struggled mightily and managed to push him off. Then she staggered away, as if under a great new weight, and Benny slumped into the patch and cried his tears into the soil. That's not a bad thing, but I did have to move him when I felt the selfish roots note his distraction and start towards him.

She took my gemflower, he said, when I helped him to his feet. *My first flower, and she took it.* His hands were empty.

I said: *there'll be many others.*

And so there will, for him.

I wonder if that's the pain he chooses, now, to find his final push to the jewels. Easily done, it's powerful, shockingly so, and here comes the vine, and the flower, which is a deep red this time, thrilling and angry. He takes it and watches the vine die back, its job done. He smiles at me. A real smile.

Let me never get used to such gifts. Let me never take his dear face for granted, or lose the pleasure of his talent, or my own. Let me give him everything and find that it only makes more for me.

In the wake of my failure, he is a steady presence, patting my hand. He looms over me, but his shadow is a good place to be.

I have given him most of the patch already, but I've long kept a little corner for myself. Well, maybe the time has come to give that up too; to admit total defeat. And then what? To walk out into the world, perhaps, and see its lies for myself? Travel beyond the market on the doorstep of the dome? I could go now, while I still have a pocket of flowers and the use of my legs, although it takes a while to get them warmed up to the task of walking.

Even so, this has been my first year in which not one vine has reached the jewels in the roof. My plants will no longer make that final push. I have lifted up my arms, and still they ignore me. They are perfectly happy as they are and have no interest in what is above them.

Benny says, 'You've been trying too hard for too long. Recover your strength and stop worrying about it. Isn't it market day? I'll fetch you a treat.'

He knows it's market day. Gretel and the others are already out there, trading and talking and giving me the space that defeat creates. Why does he phrase it as a question? As usual, he hides his real thoughts away. 'No, no, don't waste your flowers on me,' I tell him.

'That's not a waste. What else are flowers for?'

That is a good question. Flowers buy our essentials, that's true. We grow to buy to grow. At some point one of us will make enough to give up the life of the patch before we're too old to enjoy it. It'll take young legs to find truth out there, if it exists. If anyone could do it, it would be Benny. I should give him all my saved flowers before they are wasted away on my upkeep.

Or perhaps Marty was wrong, and everything out there is true, and the lies lurk in here. Right in this dome, all the time. I've had this thought more and more recently. I hate it, but I keep having it. No wonder my plants won't grow.

'Who built the domes?' says Benny, suddenly.

'The first growers.' I retell the old story, the one I used to recite at night so he could take it into sleep.

'No, I mean really,' he says, with impatience. He shifts his weight, stares at the jewels above. 'Why would the growers have built domes, anyway? How would they have known what was needed first, dome or plant? The moment I think about it, it all makes no sense.'

'Who knows what the first growers did or thought?' But I find I want to give him answers. I've always had answers for him before, when he asked for things to believe in. This is different. This time, he asks to prove me wrong. He does this more and more, thinking we are separated by stories rather than brought together.

'We do these things without understanding them,' he says. 'You've given your whole life to it.'

'Not yet I haven't!'

He chuckles. 'No. Not yet.'

'If there are answers, I don't think they're here,' I suggest. Let him take the flowers, all the flowers, and go. Let him not stay to watch me wither.

'I'm not sure that's true,' he muses, and I can't think of any question or answer to give to that.

I could not have been clear enough, loud enough, and I did not see he was in danger from the most basic, most simple of things, and even though this was his first lesson it was forgotten, how could he have forgotten it? I do not understand, cannot begin to make sense of his body and the plant wrapped around his legs, making its way inside –

'It was my choice,' he says, quietly, when I manage to control myself.

Gretel is holding me, her arms around my waist, and the others have gathered around. Such a small band, and he is the pride of us all.

Now he is dead. He will be dead as soon as the strands reach his brain. They will need no encouragement to grow; none of his talent, or my tricks and techniques. They will use him as their food, and enter his brain, and suck it dry. I can't bear it.

'I promise you,' he says, 'this is a good thing.'

That, I cannot stand for. It is for no good and serves no purpose. It is a waste of his life. I break free and shout at him; I fill the dome with my voice, and I call him all the words I know for an idiot. Then, with a hoarse throat, I tell him, 'You wanted more, yes, I saw that in you, but you could have found more. Nothing was stopping you.'

'I could have gone out into the world, you mean? But what I want is here.'

'You want this? This slow death that leads nowhere? This plant won't even reach past the top of your head. It will impregnate no jewels, make no flowers.'

'What I want is not up there. It's down here.'

Is he looking at me? No, he moves his gaze to his feet, deep in the soil. He planted himself deliberately.

'It is already talking to me. I can hear it.'

'The dirt talks to you. And what does it say, Benny? Tell me what it says.'

He keeps his eyes cast down, and he whispers, 'I can't understand it yet. But it won't be long.'

So I feed him and I water him and I watch him die.

When the first tendrils sprout from his mouth, they put out those curious buttresses and brace themselves on the skin of his cheeks. They look strong and determined. He can no longer talk, and there is no way to tell if he has finally found what he wanted to know. Still, I think I see something in his eyes that once only showed when he smiled true. I think I will choose to call it contentment. Or perhaps his mind has already been taken by the plant. Either way, it won't be long.

We grow to sell to grow to buy to grow. Where do we grow to? Is there a place we strive to reach?

He always was a boy good at lying for the benefit of others. That final soft release, the close of the eyes, the long sigh: if it is for my benefit, I thank him.

But if he had lived for my benefit, he never would have let the plant have him at all.

The plant does its best, but once it has used up the food of the brain it cannot sustain itself. It quests hard for the jewels, but when Benny's body falls it collapses with him, and that is the end of that.

'What will you do?' says Gretel, after we push the remains all the way into the dirt. Such fertile soil.

'I have it in mind to tell his mother.'

'You know where she is?'

I point to the door. The market, the road beyond. I'll know her when I see her. I suspect she'll understand this loss but hardly thank me for bringing it, and making her feel it all over again.

Who am I kidding?

I won't find her. It must be a vast world and she could be anywhere within it. She'll be telling her own lies in her own way, because that's what we all do, in and out of domes. We make the act of living easier when we can, with their telling. Finding Benny's mother is a lie to help me find my courage. And it's told for the benefit of Gretel, too, who shakes her head and cries at the thought of being here without me but will not leave. She was always late to the patch and early to the market, but it turns out those were just ways to pretend to herself that she was not stuck. Now, she admits it. She will not come with me.

I hug her long and hard, and she says, 'I have flowers saved. You take them.'

'I have more than enough. You spend them. Spend them on the things you like.'

'There isn't much I like. I don't care for growing, not in the way you did. The market has its distractions, but still. I never did like anything but you,' she says, her eyes wide; I think she has surprised herself with these words. 'And that boy you bought. I did like that boy.'

In the end, there's only people. Benny should have looked there. Not up at the jewels, not down at the soil. People. There are plenty of them out there. I clutch my hands to my pocket and make my sore old legs move. They'll be fine once they get going.

Let me get far from this place, and let me find a way to look down on the dome to see its curve for myself. Let me understand how my whole life could be so small. Let me ask the people I meet on the way if they know any stories about the growers, and the purpose of growing. I wonder if what they tell me will be real, and true.

Beast

There are roads that are only straight to the eye. They are going someplace far away, that's the feeling; the curve can't be sensed, not by humans. At the end of the journey, it's a surprise to find that no real distance has been travelled, and I arrive as I left. Unchanged. Full circle.

Beast knows me well enough to proceed without instruction, beyond one word: *Go.*

It's as close as I get to having a co-parent at these moments, imagining that the companion reads my thoughts somehow, the Beast as a person, and I resent that and lean into it. It is indispensable at the end of another long day. How was parenting done before vees existed? I think of my parents, and their parents, and the long line of existence that leads to here.

Beast commands the vee onto the city circular.

This road is ancient, a relic from an earlier age made anew. It would have been crammed with people travelling to buildings to work, in jobs that involved their hands, their physical presence. Commuters. Crashes were commonplace, and it would have taken hours to cut a mangled body from the jagged metal, the shards of glass. Meanwhile, others would drive around the mess and complain that they were being delayed. Top speeds could not be obtained, and people craved that, even breaking the law to get the thrill of danger, the illusion of escape. The old footage is fascinating.

Beast adjusts the windows. It knows I like them just a few degrees up from opaque, so I can see the trees, the fields, the suggestion of the reclaimed tangled growths – land left behind where manipulated crops dominated, and fires and floods wiped it all clean. It's peaceful, natural. At least to me. Am I seeing it honestly? How can I witness this world I'm inside? I can only see through the vee's tint. I must trust this the best road.

These thoughts. I'm in a safe place to have them. That's why they bother me, refuse to be banished. Beast will go around and around on the circular all night, and Mati will sleep, I will sleep, but not before these thoughts have run their course. I talked to Beast about them, and it said this is part of the baby blues. The thoughts always bother me at around this time. Beast called it my *midnight shade of melancholy*. It has a poetic side. I check the dashboard display. 11.52pm. Perfect. And the readout of Mati is sublime beside the time. Stable: heart, lungs, REM state.

'Breathing,' I murmur, and Beast amplifies the snuffling sound, putting it through the front speakers only, by my head and feet. At first, I thought she was always on the verge of a cold, but none has materialised. Her nostrils are so tiny; the tubes that lead from them must be as fine as flower stems. She breathes. Beast gives me a moment, safe in that sound, before letting it fade away.

'Thanks,' I say.

Beast knows better than to talk, but it flicks up the interior sidelight on my side, just once, as an acknowledgement.

More and more people are choosing vees without windows. I see them on the circular sometimes, closed to the world, caught up in their own business. No, I still want to see out. Not only at what can be projected. Not just at beauty. Ugliness must mean something; it feels like my duty to witness it, sometimes. How can I make the world a better place for Mati if I can't see it?

The questions that must follow — how can I change the world by looking at it? And what makes me think I'm looking at the real world, if I've never set foot in it?

But this must be real. We're approaching the part of the circular where the trees peter out and the barrier becomes a fence, broken in parts, peeled back from the corners. Beyond it I glimpse lights, very bright, and old vees stacked high on metal scaffolds, sorted by colour and shape. I have, in the past, seen figures amid the vees. People who have opted out. I don't see any today, and then I'm past, and passing only trees. The broken fence will come around again in forty minutes. That's the baby route.

'Rock mode,' I say, and Beast starts the slow oscillation, steering left and right. My chair tilts in time. Soon, I'll sleep. When I wake, we'll be parked up outside our home again, and both Mati and I will be ready for a day of living, learning, loving. Up for experiences, such as Sing and Clap. Old songs, such as *The Wheels on the Bus*. Imagine that – a bumpy bus, all squeezed in together. There is a company that does mystery tours to reclaimed picnic spots; they have the shell of a big red bus, and a conductor. Maybe I'll sign us up, Mati and me.

In the afternoon, I'll work. Put in my three hours while Mati spends time with Tulip in her room. Tulip is a good addition to the household, fitting right in, doing what needs to be done. It never oversteps boundaries, and it doesn't speak in the vee, not ever. The important thing is that Mati and I make our bond first, before she gets settled into AI living.

'Breathing,' I murmur, and there it is, in out, in out. I could ask Beast to rotate the chair, so I can look on her face, in the cot, on the back. What if I wake her? It's so hard to get her to sleep, so hard. Only the vee does the trick.

'Put her up,' I say, and there she is, scrunched up in her dreams, layered in the protections of this life. She is unbearably lucky. Imagine refusing these benefits, deciding to reject it all, live on the back roads, commandeer the old and broken vees. I asked Beast about it, and it said it had no relevant information. Of course not. If you choose to live off grid, there's no way you would want to be a figure on a graph. The whole idea is not to be knowable, isn't it?

I don't understand how it all works.

Nobody does, maybe.

I have this theory that I can't comprehend the outside because I'm always on the inside. It's a question of dimension. The walls of my house, of my vee. And Beast, too, is a wall.

I named it while I was in my fairy tale phase. I was Beauty. Everyone called me that. I had the dresses, the songs, even a toy digital mirror that showed me things, people. Safe online content. I would say: show me the world, and it would put up a scene of the Taj Mahal, or some other grand sight. I didn't understand the Taj Mahal had once existed. It was simply another story from the past. My mirror got broken – I left it on the stairs and my father trod on it, in a hurry to get to the door. He was a cycling nut, and he paid for access to all the best routes but had to be there at certain times to avoid paying super-premium. The graveyard slots. He was always running late. The family vee would drop him at the start of one route or another. Cycle so far in the allotted time, then call for the vee to take him back. He doesn't leave the house now, but he has a stationary cycle in a screenroom. He keeps fit.

Beast was a kind voice when the mirror broke. 'Let's order another,' it said. I was adamant – how could another be ordered? Surely it was unique. A magical object. Beast agreed with me. 'You're right,' it said. 'One and only. Like you.'

I needed a friend. Tulip will be the same for Mati one day. She'll choose a name, supplant the Tulip placeholder. But I think it will always be Tulip, first and foremost, to me.

Before Beast was Beast, it was Alex, apparently. That was the generic name for the technology. It seemed strange to me that my parents didn't have their own name for it, but they were a different generation, trying to keep it all at arm's length, distrustful of what it might all mean. *Where does this road lead?* my father said. I can tell him now: it leads nowhere. It goes around and around in ever-steady circles.

Other vees are rocking, too. We weave in time, in and out, like the making of a long, strong rope. Beast is in constant conversation with them, keeping timings and tempo under their management. Speed, velocity. Parents and babies, soothed to sleep, and the wheels on the bus go round and round, and they are the safest little children in the world right now, whatever the world means.

Something from the Garden

There will, eventually, be darkness.

'Are you thinking of marrying him?' says my auntie.

'I'm merely in it for the sex,' I tell her.

'Thank goodness for that! I don't think he's the marrying type.'

The formal garden is peaceful, bathed in the last light of the longest day, and I choose a red rose to cut from the bushes. I like to catch them at the perfect moment, just past the bud but not quite yet in the act of advertising. I bend and twist the stem until it breaks, and I strip it of its thorns, breaking each one off in turn, letting them fall to the grass. Maybe they'll stick into my auntie later; she will potter around this place in bare feet. Well, one bare foot. The left. She wears an immaculate pink dress, with a sash tied at the back, like a little girl taken to a tea party. The right foot is encased in a silk slipper bearing grass stains. But the left foot is always out on display, the big toe turned inwards, the bunion standing proud.

'If I wanted to, I'd marry him.' I don't like the idea she's picked up that I'm essentially unlovable. Perhaps it's a deflection. I don't think anybody ever loved her.

'Is that for me?' she says shyly, ready to curtsy and accept her rose.

'Absolutely not. You shouldn't be out here too much longer. Go in and get ready for bed.'

Her shoulders slump, and she wanders away: not towards the house, but around it, taking up her usual circles. She and I both know that the night won't come yet, and there's still much to do.

In the hall sits my love, on the bottom step of the grand staircase, his elbows on his knees, his palms pressed together as if in prayer. I've never thought of him as the praying type before.

He looks up and says, 'It's you.'

'It's me.' I cross the chequered floor, tiles of black and white, to reach him. He shifts on the stair so I can squeeze in between his reassuring body and the banister. I'm soft, small, compressed. I love the way he makes me feel like a celestial object viewed through the wrong end of a telescope. I realise I will marry him, if he asks. At this moment.

He opens his pressed-together palms and gives me confirmation that he wasn't praying – see, I do know him – but holding something. It's sitting in his left palm. A silver ring.

I hold out the rose.

He takes it in his right hand, as if weighing the two objects. Then he focuses his attention on the folded heart of the rose, where the smallest petals curve and come together. It reminds me of my baby, who emerged in silence, as red as the flower and open-mouthed in aghast wonder. She was folded up tight too. It took her hours to uncurl.

'Do you remember?' he says.

'Absolutely.'

'And then there was the thing with the –' He can't tame the words, but he doesn't need to for my benefit. I laugh at the memory, and he laughs too.

The ring still sits on his palm.

I would look at him under my lashes, and ask for it, but all I can think of is my auntie and her coquettish ways that have stuck to her so long after she should have shaken them off. *Is that for me?* So I don't mention it, and he doesn't either. The light of the sun streams through the long windows. I have so much to do, but I can't move from him, not yet. I want him: his laugh, his memories of me, his ring.

I put my head on his shoulder. He hums a familiar tune. If I'm using him for sex, I'm not doing a good job of it. But I want to imagine I am, so I say, 'Meet me upstairs for a quickie?'

'Really?' he says, his eyebrows raised. I've managed to surprise him. He acts as if I've never propositioned him before, and that annoys me in its erasure: that time in the car, that one trip to the seaside, in the dunes. He's meant to be storing all these events for me.

I sit up straight. 'You don't have to, if you're too busy.'

'No, I want to, sure. A quickie. Tell you what, take this and I'll see you up there.' He holds out the ring.

'Are you sure?' I ask him.

'Just to hold on to,' he says. 'For now.'

I take the ring and I put it on. It fits. But it doesn't mean what I thought it would mean. I don't feel different.

He plays with the rose, touching the petals that are already curling back from the centre. The beauty of it will soon be lost. At least a ring is permanent; I think I've got the better deal. But it's also true that nothing lasts forever. Not even today. The night will fall and I'll be in bed with my lover – that's the promise we made, which has nothing to do with rings and roses.

I stand up, and abandon his clarity. 'See you later,' I say, as casually as I can, and I take the stairs to the next thing that must be done.

Here lies my baby, not quite asleep, because there's only so much blackout blinds can do. She's drowsy, though, even with that slice of light sneaking into the nursery, cutting its way across the foot of the cot.

I lean over the bars and whisper to her, words that make perfect nonsense: *it's the tone of voice that's important*, someone said to me, once. It feels like old wisdom, which is the kind I like.

She meets my look with a grave glance of her own, but I see no recognition in her filmy eyes. Of course, she's too young for that: we have to make our memories. Who knows what will become her first memory? My own is of this very room, lying still, watching motes in sunlight. That meandering drift of a thousand specks, like microscopic creatures in a sea. I was adrift amongst them, my only company. Nothing can ever quite feel real in a nursery.

I want her first memory to be a good one. Better than mine. Not a memory of loneliness. If only there could be a guarantee that she'd catch and hold my face in her mind, at just the right moment, full-blown in the act of loving her.

'See this face?' I tell her. 'This face will always take care of you.'

She crumples up her eyes and mouth at the sound of my voice. Oh, don't cry, don't cry my baby. She doesn't cry. I'm relieved although I know, objectively, that she must cry sometimes. It's part of the process. It causes me pain, though, and I'm so sick of pain. The thorns that get scattered underfoot.

She settles once more. My beautiful one. There will never be another thing so perfect in this world; at least, not to me. Not today.

I slip off the silver ring and place it on her chest. She's so tiny, she can't grasp it, can't even open her fists yet for long. The ring sits between the buttons of her sky-blue Babygro. What will she give me in return? Love? I long for it, but I can't be sure. That's not how the world works, and I can't remember loving my mother, not as a gift to meet her expectations, nor as a trade for her time. Children are so selfish.

In the absence of anything better I take a toy from her cot. A stuffed rabbit. It's small and soft, it's one of many such toys that are lined up alongside her, and it feels good in my hands. I press it to my face and breathe in the smell of her that has sunk into the material. She won't even know it was hers to begin with, if I claim it now. It was one of the many presents that arrived in the first days after her birth. So many boxes came, the cards inside addressed:

To Mummy and Baby

These aren't our names, I thought, with every envelope I opened.

'I'll take care of this for you,' I tell her. 'I'll do a good job of looking after it. I'm a responsible adult now.'

She doesn't move. Her eyes are closing, closing, closed. I think she's finally about to sleep. I tiptoe away, determined not to wake her; there's nothing as delicate as the senses of a baby. Just one sound, and she'll stir and then I'll be stuck here all night, singing all the same old songs. But no, I've made it to the door, and I can move on to my next task. There are still so many things to get done.

My gramps can always be found in the billiards room.

I confess I don't know the rules for billiards; in truth, I've always resisted the information, thinking it might spoil the magic of watching him play. He lines up his cue and strikes the white ball so that it hits the black, and the black travels at a sedate, slowing speed to the corner pocket where it sinks. He turns to the rack on the mantelpiece, beside the clunky carriage clock, and slides the pointer along the numbers to record his score. He only ever plays alone: *you make the best competition for yourself*, he once told me.

'Unexpected maintenance,' he says, as he chalks his cue. 'It's falling down, one piece at a time. A quote for the roof, remind me, and tree surgery, that's necessary. Trees and their growing and dying back. It's not the branches you need to worry about as much as the roots, though, disrupting the foundations.'

'I'll remind you,' I say, knowing it'll never stay in my head. It doesn't matter. I can't believe this house will ever fall down, no matter how he worries.

'Bunkins!' he says, his sharp eyes falling to the stuffed rabbit. 'I remember Bunkins from when you were little. You wouldn't be parted from him. Where did you find him?'

'Upstairs. In the nursery. But he's not mine – he's brand new.' It comes to me – I've left the ring on my baby's chest. How could I have been so stupid? I'm a terrible parent, she could swallow it, it could stick in her throat, she could somehow manage to pick it up or roll on it or I don't know anything, anything, I've failed to protect her from herself, I must get back to the nursery and make it right–

My gramps reads it all on my face: 'Now, now, now, what's wrong, my little one?' He puts down the cue and comes to me, folds me up in his arms, and he's right. I am still the little one with a stuffed bunny in my hands and tears in my eyes for a hurt he thinks he can take away.

'I'm a terrible...mother...' I tell him, in between sobs, and he strokes my hair and says, 'We're all terrible people in lots of ways, angel, not to worry. Not to worry.' He wraps me up in the smell of cough sweets and wood shavings. Why should he carry such scents on him? I don't understand how age impregnates the body and changes it all for its own purpose. And in the middle of that thought I realise that my guilt has lost it sharp edge. My need to return to the nursery and retrieve the ring is passing. It's funny how quickly the worst emotions, born of the most painful mistakes, leave us. Perhaps that's what age is — the quiet adjustment to the weight of blame.

My gramps lets me go and steps back. He looks long into my face, and I into his. His assessing eyes are almost lost in the folds of his face, but not quite. Not quite. I wonder what he sees.

'There now,' he says. 'That's better.'

'It is,' I say. 'How did you do that?'

'It's the tone of voice that's important.'

He's right again, of course. It's the softness that age brings to his voice, so easy to mistake as wisdom.

'I made you something,' he says, as he returns to the billiard table and picks up his cue. 'It's on the sideboard.'

Yes, there's a new object on the long table beside the mantelpiece, where the framed photographs of the long family line are kept, white faces schooled into serious poses amidst the grey of the past. It's a little wooden cross, crudely made, but varnished so it shines. Is that why my gramps smells of wood? I picture him hard at work on this for me, cutting and planing and measuring his work.

'Thank you,' I say. 'I'll cherish it.' I put down the stuffed rabbit and take up the cross. It's rough, and lighter than I thought it would be.

'Good, good. Get along, then,' he tells me, and I do as I'm told, even though I hate the next obligation. Still, what can be done? It must be completed, and I've never failed in my duty. I pocket the cross and set off for the cellar.

Down in the cellar, down where the sun can't go and the wine that can't be drunk is racked and numbered, lives my twin.

'Oh God,' she says, when she hears my footsteps. All is dark until I light the candelabra, waiting in the usual alcove for me, set back in the damp bricks. The light throws long shadows over her face, her white body that twists away from me. She is so very ugly.

'I hate this process as much as you do,' I tell her, and she says, 'I very much fucking doubt that.' It's better when she swears and shows her anger; it makes it easier to turn the wheel, so I get on with it, and crank it round, pulling at the spokes until the rope around her hands tightens, and stretches her out upon her rack. She screams. She uses terrible words, awful words. How I despise her. How grateful I am that she's decided not to beg for mercy this time.

'Come on, come on,' I mutter. It's become my mantra in this place. Let time move on, let this be done, but she won't give in easily, she won't submit. I put all my effort into the wheel and strain, strain, until – there. A crack. It's not loud but I feel it through the spokes, and I know my job is done. I let the wheel go and step close to look at her body, dangling upon the rack, the fight in her spent. She's naked apart from one shoe, which she has always refused to give up. A silk slipper. I suppose she clings to the idea of walking out of here. Well, don't we all.

I search for the new injury, and find her skin has split in the hollow under her ribcage. A clean line across her white stomach. No blood.

This bit is always the same. I have to check. I put my fingers to the wound. She's the same inside. Just the black. She winces at my touch, and sucks in her breath. 'No,' she says, 'No no no,' and I tell her gently, 'I have to.' I reach inside, and probe the darkness. Empty. There is nothing inside her. Nothing at all.

I remove my fingers. 'Done,' I say, and she breathes out. The cut will have healed by the next time I see her, forming a fine scar. She has so many of them, all over her torso, her face, her limbs, her hands and feet. I have tortured her everywhere.

'Oh God,' she whispers, again. She's big on God. Perhaps that's the prerogative of those in pain. I remember the cross I carry, and I pull it out.

'It's a present,' I tell her, and she says, 'For me?' so eagerly that I can't bear to tell her no, no, it's my present, from my family. I stand on tiptoe and put it in one of her hands, stretched high above her head. Her fingers fold around it with such delight, even though it means she can't see it, can't ever put it down. It will grow heavy, surely. Still, we cling to what we must.

'You look terrible,' I tell her.

'Isn't it getting dark?' she says.

'Surely. It's Midsummer Eve, but it will get dark eventually. It has to.'

'It always does.'

It's good to end on a note of agreement. I would leave it there, but as I walk away she calls out, 'Bring me something from the garden next time, won't you? Please? For old times' sake.'

What harm could it do? I'll cut something fresh, something sweet and summery, so she can be sure of the time of year. I try to fix this task in my memory, but there are so many tasks to get done, and the night is close now. It's coming. I'll never get everything done. But I could go now, to the garden, and get it done. Sooner is better than later. I blow out the candelabra and leave her behind me. I'm awash with the relief of the hard task done properly.

I cut through the empty living room to avoid the hall and climb out of the window to reach the garden. In the distance I can see my aunt dancing, twirling, her head thrown back, her hair loose. She thinks I'm unlovable, but she's wrong. I'm certain of it.

She's in the formal rose garden, so I'll have to speak to her, and have another one of those interminable conversations about my life choices. If I'm lucky it won't last long. The light is dusky and intense; surely these are the final moments before sunset? I set off at speed, half-running to reach the roses. So many tasks to get through, but even Midsummer Eve will end and leave so much undone. Still, I must believe that there will, eventually, be darkness.

At Night, the Road

When I was young the night was only a cobweb: spun strands that separated me from the land where stories lived. I could push through it, my hands before my small cold face. I would creep from my bed and out of the house, and run fast through the dark, breath streaming, the stretch of lawn glittering, the grass wet between my toes. I wanted to reach the fence by the treeline: beyond that lay the woods, and then the road.

The road is still there, and a different kind of monster travels on it now. I hear they have plans to make it into a motorway. So many headlights will shine; whoever owns what was once my house will live in a place of permanent bright light and sounds. Horns honking, and shining metal eyes.

Let's be honest: there is less attention paid to the night now anyway. I see people out so late, and still working, shopping, ensconced in electricity. If all the lights went out they would freeze, not knowing what to do first. They would be still and sacrificial in their fear.

Not me. I know what it is to move through the black. I have chased tales with my eyes closed, using only desire and luck to place my feet.

I was so young when I found the strength to turn the key in the back door, and I remember how the iron grated in the lock and bruised my fingers. It took both hands. Then I was out, moving fast. Not to be away from my house, which I loved, and not to escape my parents, whom I took for granted as existing, like the house, in a state of permanence. It was only that the darkness changed everything, and I wanted to know it, and to be changed in accordance.

I wanted to have meaning.

I still want it, but I have learned to chase it with less vigour. I am afraid of what a tumble in the dark would do to me, and I suspect my luck has run out, and perhaps also my desire. I've lived for decades in the suspicion that I'm no longer what I was, protecting myself, folding inwards and looking for the place where meaning lives within my own thoughts. But soon the road will be transformed and so I must admit to myself that I've been a coward all these years, and this is my last chance.

I wake, in the city. I kneel up in my bed and crack open the curtains, and find no surprises beyond, on the street, where every white line is visible, painted straight. I can't bear it, to think of this mundanity reaching into the woods and stealing away my road. It will be gone soon, gone for good, and then I'm moving, getting clothes, picking up car keys, and I'm driving back home.

Stupid, I say to myself, as I journey. But my own voice is meaningless, outside myself, and I won't turn around.

I'm at my old house.

I turn off the car lights so that I won't wake those strangers who are deep in sleep inside. I turn off the engine and wait, half expecting to see myself, small me, emerge from the front door, fingers still smarting from the key in the lock.

That was then, and that has gone. I remember how big the lawn seemed, everything seemed, but everything is miniaturised by modern life: the lawn does not stretch away to the treeline. It is only a well-kept stretch of a few adult strides.

I get out of the car, and walk to the wooden fence, in disrepair. It is the original, and with that thought the past finds me. Here is the magic I remember, for suddenly I'm unsure again, and the tall trunks, the patterns of the branches beyond, shrinks me to small fingers, small toes. I climb the fence and move into the weavings of the night. The cobwebs surround me. The strands cover my face, my hair, and I push through them, head out, moving with my thoughts set on the road.

The road did not lead anywhere, once upon a time. It was a path from the place of stories, travelling nowhere and everywhere, as stories do. In one of my childhood night-time travels I found the sudden smoothness of it underfoot, and then the trees shrank back, and I had the sense of being open, exposed, although the darkness stole all sight. Then I became aware of their approach. It wasn't a sound. It was the smell – on the breeze – the smell of the turning of pages of old books. Age, and crumbling pages, from which the monsters had slipped free.

I shivered in my nightdress. I closed my eyes. They would do me no good. I breathed in the smell, and then heard the tread of their feet and the call of their voices, approaching: a cascade of sound, like a river, with only that moment's notice before there was the icy shock of their presence around me, over me. I was drenched in them; I could not breathe because of them. I understood then that nothing is conjured from thin air. Inspiration, imagination – flows into the words from a source of which we only catch droplets. But the river leads back to its mouth. It springs from an ocean of creation.

I want the ocean. I want to no longer grasp for droplets, to chase these creatures through the language of others and then to force them into my own words. I want to find them, and to make them take me along.

I don't remember how, as a cold, lost child, I got home that night. But I remember how I wrote the next day, filling pages with the creatures from the road. Not beings with arms, heads, legs, but rather things that stretched the limits of my mind. I read my writings back, later, and realised I had not captured the creatures at all. I hid the pages away, embarrassed by my efforts.

As I push through the trees once more, I realise that perhaps these years of looking within for the monsters have not been cowardice after all, but practice. I have learned a craft, and now I might even be ready to do justice to what I find on the road tonight. I push on, push on. I feel the prickle of the rough carpet of leaves and twigs underfoot, and the sensation of squashing soft flowers where they have erupted. I hold my hands in front of me, touching the bark of the trunks, steering myself onwards, waiting for the smoothness, and the scent of old books opened. I head for the road, before it is gone for good.

About the Author

Aliya Whiteley's strange novels and novellas explore genre, and have been shortlisted for multiple awards including the Arthur C. Clarke award, BFS and BSFA awards, and a Shirley Jackson award. Her short fiction has appeared in many places including *Beneath Ceaseless Skies, F&SF, Strange Horizons, McSweeney's Internet Tendency, Lonely Planet* and *The Guardian*. She also writes a regular non-fiction column for *Interzone* magazine. She lives in West Sussex, UK.

ALSO FROM NEWCON PRESS

Polestars 1: Strange Attractors – Jaine Fenn

First full collection from the award-winning author of innovative science fiction and off-kilter fantasy; features her finest short stories, selected by the author, drawn from more than two decades of publication, including the BSFA Award-winning "Liberty Bird", a Hidden Empire story, and a new tale, "Sin of Omission", written specifically for this collection.

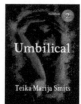

Polestars 2: Umbilical – Teika Marija Smits

Debut collection from one of the finest short story writers to emerge on the genre scene in recent years. Her storytelling relies on keen observation of the world and people around her interpreted through the lens of her imagination, dancing between science fiction, realism, and horror.

Polestars 3: The Glasshouse – Emma Coleman

Contemporary tales of rural horror and dark fantasies steeped in folklore from one of genre fiction's best kept secrets. A young divorcee relocates to a quaint rural hamlet but is mystified by the hostility of her neighbours…A man discovers an item in a junkshop that puts him in fear of his life… An impresario dispenses justice while performing as a magician…

Polestars 4: Our Savage Heart – Justina Robson

The first collection in twelve years from one of the UK's most respected and inventive writers of science fiction and fantasy. 100,000 words of high quality fiction, that gathers together the author's finest stories from the past decade, including a brand new piece written especially for this collection.

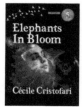

Polestars 5: Elephants in Bloom – Cécile Cristofari

Debut collection from a French author who has been making a name for herself with regular contributions to *Interzone* and elsewhere. Providing a fresh perspective on things, Cécile's fiction reflects her love of the natural world and concern for its future. Contains her finest previously published stories and a number of brand new tales that appear for the first time.